Catch a

CATCH A WHISPER

by

Patricia Fawcett

To Frances and Amanda with many thanks…

CHAPTER ONE

Preston, Lancashire early 1930's

"Where are you off to then, Nessa Cookson, in your Sunday best?"

"Never you mind," she said, rushing past Tony and his pals who were lounging about on the street corner. She heard their whistles and laughter and would have turned and given them what for but she had no time today for the likes of Tony Walsh who thought he was Haydock Street's answer to Clark Gable. If she didn't get a move on, she would be late for the interview up at Ruby House and that would never do.

Her feet were killing her because the shoes did not really fit but the frock made up for that. The frock was beautiful; emerald green satin with a cape of frills at the shoulder and a row of little satin-covered buttons all the way down the back. It was a snug fit though because Nessa had more of a shape than her sister Lizzie who had been given this precious frock by one of the ladies at the house she worked in.

"You look lovely, our Nessa, you're my pretty one, you are," her mum had said, when she finished with the fiddly doing up of the buttons. "Mrs Bamber says the job is as good as yours so all you have to do is answer her questions and don't be cheeky. And go easy with that scent because you don't want her to think you're loose and make sure you're back before our Lizzie. I don't want her knowing that you've borrowed the frock. You know what she's like."

"It's all right, mum," Nessa said with a smile. She got herself into a panic, did her mum, and she had been in a right old stew from the start this morning. They hadn't dared tell Dad about this so they had to wait until he was off before they could get started.

After her mother had fussed her off, she took a moment in the privacy of the back yard to execute a cupid's bow with the red lipstick that her other sister Maggie had got from one of the flightier mill-girls. Now, as she approached Ruby House, the gracious red-brick home of the mill-owner George Whitlock, she wondered if that was a mistake because she remembered that Mrs Bamber was a member of the Temperance Movement and they were a right miserable lot and didn't believe anybody should have any fun.

She was hot and bothered when she finally arrived at the back door where she was told to sit on a bench in the servants' corridor and wait. The aroma of something cooking drifted around mingling with the smell of lavender furniture polish. Taking a seat, she saw that she had a blooming great blister on her foot now but that couldn't be helped.

With a sigh of relief that she had made it in time, she took stock of the girl sitting beside her who was also up for the job. This girl was pale with freckly skin, even her eyes were pale and her lips were free of lipstick. She was wearing a hat too, her red hair tucked neatly beneath it and carrying gloves. She was wearing subdued lilac and it suddenly dawned on Nessa that her emerald green satin frock was more suited to an evening soiree. She was not sure what that was exactly but she had heard it talked about in one of the pictures she had seen at the picture house in town. At an evening soiree you would look beautiful and carry a gorgeous silk evening bag and maybe have a holder for your cigarette. A man with smouldering brown eyes would lean into you and offer you a light and you would smile prettily at him and…

"Have you been running?" the girl asked. "You look flushed."

Nessa put a hand up to her dark brown hair, fluffing it up and feeling the dampness at her neck. "I ran the last bit because I thought I was going to be late," she said. "And it's uphill all the way. It's fair puffed me out."

"You get a grand view from up here. You can see the park and the river from the front," the girl said with a little sniff. "I'm Marjorie. What's your name?"

"Nessa." She caught the glance Marjorie gave her and felt the need to explain. "It's my sister's frock," she said. "We haven't told her I'm wearing it and she'll go daft if she finds out."

"Why didn't you ask her? You shouldn't take things without asking," the girl added with another sniff of disapproval.

"You don't ask my sister Lizzie for favours," she told her as, out in the hall, a clock daintily chimed the hour.

"I don't have any sisters," Marjorie said, making a point of handling her white cotton gloves. "Haven't you got a hat then?"

"I left it at home," Nessa said, thinking about the black jersey cap of Maggie's that Maggie had left out especially for her. It messed up her hair and she was proud of her long curly hair and wanted to show it off. In any case, it wasn't any of Marjorie's business whether or not she had a hat.

Nessa decided she didn't really like this girl who had in the space of a few minutes pointed out she was both hatless and flushed but she smiled at her anyway.

"Do you go to the pictures much?" Marjorie said, hardly pausing for breath before carrying on. "I went to see The Blue Angel last week with my boyfriend. Do you have a boyfriend?"

Seeing the other girl's smug expression, Nessa thought about fibbing for a minute before shaking her head. The last time she went to the pictures it was with a boy to watch a horrible cowboy film where everybody was shooting everybody else. There was a lot of booing and hissing in the audience all the way through but, sitting in the back row with him, she had experienced her first kiss though. When Maggie found out, she was told not to do it again until she was older. Boys take advantage, she warned, and Nessa had to watch it because she was pretty. Nessa took note of what Maggie said for Maggie was seventeen years older and like a second mum.

She shivered at the thought of getting into trouble which had happened to a few girls her age and moistened her lips, wishing now she hadn't used the red lipstick because she caught the snooty glance Marjorie gave her. She considered wiping it off but then she would get her white handkerchief dirty and she only had the one proper hankie.

"Oh, look, there's William Whitlock himself crossing the hall," Marjorie whispered, nudging her.

The door to the hall was ajar and they watched as the young man strode across the hall towards the staircase. All they could see was the back of him, tall and dark haired, walking briskly, footsteps loud and clear.

"He'll take over the mill one day," Marjorie informed her, keeping her voice low. "He has a sister older than him and he lost his mum when he was a little lad so there's just the three of them, Mr Whitlock himself, Mr William and Miss Martha."

"I know," Nessa said, thinking she could tell Marjorie a thing or two about the Whitlock family for her mother was privy to all the house and mill gossip. According to the women in the weaving shed, Martha Whitlock, William's spinster sister, sometimes peeped in, looking round as if she owned the place which she did, more or less. She didn't hang around though for the weaving shed was no place for a lady to linger. They could drop a bomb next door and the weavers wouldn't know. They had to lip-read or use sign language and after a while it affected their hearing but Martha Whitlock never stayed long enough for it to affect hers. They had her down as a snotty madam but, to their satisfaction, she was fat with a face like the backend of a Blackpool tram.

"Oh my gracious, he's coming back this way," Marjorie said, digging her fingers into Nessa's arm. "Don't look."

Catching her alarm, Nessa averted her eyes but, as the footsteps came nearer, the sound carrying on the tiled floor, she could not help but sneak a look. And, to her astonishment, he just happened to be looking at her and, even though she looked quickly away, heart pounding, she caught his sudden smile.

And that was that.

It was as shattering as the bullet that killed her Uncle Alf during the war, hammering into her, making her catch her breath, lodging deep inside. A girl of sixteen, she fell in love with the tall, dark-haired twenty one year old.

William… She whispered the name and thought how wonderful it would be to be his wife, to be Mrs William Whitlock, to be somebody. How wonderful it would be to come in the front door of Ruby House dressed in a beautiful gown, throw off her feather boa and her white kid evening gloves and take the softly carpeted grand stairs instead of the cold stone steps that led from the servants' corridor.

How wonderful it would be.

Called in to see the housekeeper shortly afterwards, she was in a little world of her own so that Mrs Bamber, lips pursed, had to repeat some questions. Nessa knew then that she had her down as dozy and so, with a capable looking Marjorie, all smiles, breezing in after her, it was a lost cause.

***

She walked back home as quickly as she could even though the blister was giving her grief, taking a short cut along a street of fancier houses each with a tiny front garden and that was where, starting to run now, she bumped into Mrs Crawford, an acquaintance of her mother's whom she had to call Auntie Florence out of respect.

Hurrying, head down, she didn't notice Auntie Florence until she turned the corner and came face to face with a dead fox, its paws and head hanging around the lady's neck. She recoiled, not just at the fox but at the lady herself for she was warned to steer clear of her.

"She's a Medium," Maggie had told her, fear in her eyes. "So stay away."

"What's a Medium?"

"Never you mind, our Nessa. You'll be better off not knowing."

And when Maggie clammed up, she clammed up. However, Nessa had it drummed into her to be polite to her elders and so she stood still, breathing hard, hot and bothered once more from the running.

"Vanessa," the lady cried out, the only person in the whole world to call her by her given name. "What a surprise. What are you doing round here in a beautiful dress like that?"

"I'm on my way home. I've been up to Ruby House for an interview for a job," she told her, catching her breath and avoiding looking into the fox's dead eyes. "It's Lizzie's frock, Auntie Florence, and she doesn't know I'm wearing it and she'll kill me if she finds out so I have to get back before she does."

"She won't kill you." Auntie Florence smiled in that vague way of hers. She was from down south, a touch above them, which was why nobody dared abbreviate the name to the more usual Florrie. Nessa had no idea what a Medium was so she couldn't quite understand why her mother and most of the other women were so suspicious of her. After all, she couldn't help it if she talked a bit different from them, could she, and she had always been quite nice to Nessa in a quiet sort of way. "I'm sure your sister Lizzie has a heart of gold underneath that exterior of hers," Auntie Florence continued, adjusting the fox's legs.

"I'm not," Nessa said with a sniff. Auntie Florence might like to think the best of folks but Nessa knew Lizzie better than most and, sister or not, she didn't trust her. It was well known in the neighbourhood that Lizzie Cookson was tuppence short of a shilling.

"I won't detain you as I see you are keen to get home." She trailed a thin almost translucent hand over the material. "It's lovely and the colour suits you, my dear. It flatters your skin. Now, run along."

Haring back home now after wasting precious seconds, terrified that Lizzie would get there before her Nessa could have stopped there and then in a corner somewhere to have a good old cry but she blinked the tears away because there was no time for them. She had to stop feeling sorry for herself because she only had herself to blame, missing out on this job because she was day dreaming and she had to stop that. Maggie called her a dreamer and maybe she was but sometimes dreams come true.

Don't they?

***

Maggie was waiting for her in the back alley, looking worried.

"About time," she said, taking hold of Nessa. "Lizzie's back and in one of her moods. Mum's keeping her in the front room for a few minutes to give us chance to get you out of that frock before she sees you."

"How?" Nessa saw the old frock Maggie was holding. "I can't get undressed here. Somebody might see."

Maggie put a finger to her lips. "Auntie Nelly's out," she said. "The gate's not locked and we can get in her back-yard and change there. Auntie Nelly won't mind. Come on."

"I don't think Mrs Bamber took a shine to me," Nessa said, following Maggie through the yard gate into their next door neighbour's yard.

"Never mind Mrs Bamber," Maggie said, struggling with the buttons and helping her out of the frock. It dropped on the ground and Maggie picked it up quickly, dusting it down, and throwing the other frock at Nessa for her to get into. Maggie was thin, too thin, and pale, too pale, with big watery brown eyes and a slightly stooped posture. Dad was always telling her to stand up straight but she didn't seem able to.

"Don't worry," she said, darting a glance towards their house. "I'll get this up to the bedroom and back in the drawer without Lizzie seeing me."

"Are you sure?"

Maggie nodded, although she didn't look convinced because you never knew with Lizzie. She crept up behind you, silently, a little fiery bundle of anger as often as not. She had her dad's temper and she and Maggie did their best to keep on the right side of her. Bundling the green frock into her arms, squashing it as flat as she could, Maggie pulled Nessa back a minute.

"Mum says you had a good chance with this job. Tell me why you don't think Mrs Bamber took a shine to you."

"I wasn't taking heed of what she was saying because I saw William Whitlock," Nessa told her. "He was crossing the hall and he looked at me and he's so handsome like a film star and he has this lovely smile. He smiled at me, Maggie, he really did," she said, her eyes shining.

Maggie huffed. "He has no business smiling at you. He should know better, a gentleman like him, than smile at silly young girls and put daft ideas in their heads. I blame all those pictures you watch at the picture house. Real life is not like that, our Nessa." She shook her head, handing her a rough cloth as she looked at her. "And best wipe that lipstick off before Mum sees you."

"But Maggie…"

Maggie adjusted the plain flannel frock Nessa had put on and they paused a minute as, over the wall, they thought they heard a movement from their yard.

"Lizzie," Maggie mouthed. "You go first," she told her, Nessa lip-reading what she was saying. "I'll bring the frock."

There was thankfully no sign of Lizzie in their yard and Nessa escaped into the house leaving Maggie to follow.

***

"Nessa loves William," Lizzie chanted as they ate their tea. It was broth with dumplings and chunks of bread. There were bits of scrag end floating amongst the vegetables but Mum made sure Dad got most of those. Maggie had no appetite as usual with her chest playing up but Lizzie ate like a horse, reaching over for Maggie's dish and pouring the left over broth into her own.

"Watch your manners, our Lizzie," Harry Cookson said, mopping up the remains of his broth with a piece of bread before smiling—as he occasionally did—at his wife. He was short and broad with a strong grip and worked as a tackler at the mill where he put the fear of God into the girls.

"Our Nessa loves William," Lizzie persisted, coal-black eyes glinting with mischief as soup dribbled down her chin.

"Shut up and wipe your mouth, Lizzie," her mum said, looking at Nessa, disappointed but resigned now to her not getting the job. They hadn't breathed a word to Dad of course so he was none the wiser. "William who, anyway? Do you mean that nice red-haired lad in the next street? He's a stevedore and you could do worse than walk out with him, Nessa, but not until you're a bit older."

"No, not him," Lizzie said. "You'll never guess who she's sweet on?"

"We're eating our tea not playing guessing games," Dad said. "And I'll thank you not to talk with your mouth full."

After tea, Maggie collared the pair of them, her and Lizzie, and took them into the back yard, swearing Lizzie to everlasting silence on the subject of William Whitlock. Maggie being the oldest by a mile was the only one who could handle Lizzie, standing up to her when nobody else would.

"You shouldn't have been listening in," she told her sharply. "You're always listening in to other folk's conversations."

"What do I get if I keep quiet?" Lizzie asked, dancing about from foot to foot. In her late twenties now, she was barely five foot tall with her dad's beady black eyes, his sturdy legs and lank, black greasy hair, all in all a cruel combination.

"You get nowt," Maggie snapped. "That's called blackmail, my girl."

"I'll get you some scent, Lizzie," Nessa said softly, shaking her head at Maggie for it was all right. Lizzie was a trial, always had been, but Nessa felt sorry for her because she was slow and never given a chance. There was a girl she knew who could get fancy little blue bottles of scent. They were from Paris, she told everybody, and nobody believed that but Lizzie would.

In the event, that and a bangle from the market did the trick. Nessa put it in a box and told Lizzie it was real silver, just a little white lie because it pleased her.

"It looks a treat," she said as Lizzie slipped it over her wrist. Her hands were red and raw from all the washing up she did at the house in Ashton but all Lizzie could see was the shiny new bangle.

"I'll wear it forever and I'll be buried wearing it," she said. "Nobody else shall have it."

***

She told Lizzie that it had been a joke and that she didn't fancy that William Whitlock one little bit. He was all puffed out and cock-a-hoop and she didn't care for men like that.

"He'll end up marrying a lady," Lizzie told her, her face growing sly. "You'll just have to learn that you can't have everything you want, little sister. There's not a lot we can have, you and me. We're stuck here forever."

Maybe she was right but Nessa didn't want to believe that. One day she would prove Lizzie wrong. She thought about him that night as she lay in bed beside Maggie. Maggie wheezed with each breath and Lizzie, in the other bed, snored and snorted all night long and sometimes she even talked in her sleep.

Nessa could see the moon through the window, a sliver of a moon tonight, thinking that William could see the very same moon from his window which offered her a crumb of comfort.

It took a long time to go to sleep that night only to be woken in the early hours to find Lizzie above her, pinning her down. Maggie was dead to the world but Lizzie was wide awake, eyes blazing with anger.

Brandishing a knife which she held to Nessa's throat.

CHAPTER TWO

"I warned you, Nessa Cookson, that I'd kill you if you wore that green frock of mine," Lizzie hissed in a whisper, the blade glinting in the moonlight. "Did you think I didn't mean it? It smells of scent and the hem's mucky."

Nessa tried to struggle up, shaking Maggie but she didn't stir because she had taken an extra slug of cough medicine and a double dose of Fennings Lung Healers so she was out for the count. "Where did you get that knife? I thought Mum hid them all."

"You thought wrong."

Lizzie had gone for Maggie in a rage a few weeks back and nicked her arm with a knife and though she got a hiding from dad, she never said sorry. Lizzie never said sorry for anything.

"It's my knife and I always have it with me," Lizzie told her, smiling now but in a nasty way. "I could kill you, little sister, slit your throat and then I'd scream the place down and say some chap had got in and done it."

"They wouldn't believe you," she said, scared to move an inch now because the look in her sister's eyes was frightening. Lizzie, in one of her moods, was dangerous. Everybody in the street knew and feared her. They drew their children closer when she passed by and whispered when she was gone.

"They would believe me. After I killed you, I'd nick myself and say he did that to me when I was trying to save you. And she's asleep," she added, nodding towards Maggie. "She won't know a thing. She'll wake up and you'll be covered in blood, our Nessa, and all because you couldn't keep your hands off my best frock."

Did she detect a break in the voice? Did it matter to Lizzie that much? She never wore the frock, just took it out of the drawer, stroking and looking at it from time to time before putting it back. She had tried it on when she first got it and they had all said that she looked lovely just to make her happy.

Nessa could feel the tip of the blade on her neck, hear the heavy breathing, smell the foul smell that often surrounded her sister but surely Lizzie would never kill her, not deliberately. She loved talk of murders, did Lizzie, talking with excited eyes about the drop room at Lancaster Castle where murderers met their end. She would love to be there, she said, and see them wriggling on the end of the rope.

"All right, I did wear the frock," she confessed and, to her relief, Lizzie leaned back taking the knife with her. "It's so beautiful but it looks a lot better on you than it does on me. It's too tight for me but it fits you just right. It looks a real treat on you."

"Does it?" Lizzie looked at her strangely and Nessa could not make up her mind whether she believed her or not. The truth was it looked terrible on Lizzie, anything did, but, although she did not truly believe Lizzie would stick a knife in her, it was just as well to be on the safe side and she would fib her heart out to do that.

"It does and you mustn't do yourself down, Lizzie. You're only little and men like that," she said, struggling for something nice to say. "I'm too tall."

"You are. You think you're beautiful but you are too tall and Maggie never stops coughing so no man would fancy her. I am little and I have lovely black eyes. Don't you wish you had my eyes? Blue eyes like yours are so common and they look daft with your hair. You should have blonde hair with those eyes."

"I know. Oh, Lizzie, put that knife down and go to sleep. You'll wake Maggie and she needs her sleep."

"She's in for an early grave," Lizzie said, matter-of-factly. "That chest of hers will see her off before long. I shall live to be a hundred because I have a charmed life. I would use this," she said sliding a finger along the knife. "I might have used it already on somebody for all you know. I know how to get away with things. I don't get caught. I am cleverer than folks think and it suits me to be thought daft. Think on that, our Nessa."

Chilling words although it was no surprise because Nessa had always thought there was more to her sister than meets the eye.

She watched as Lizzie gathered up her nightgown and clambered off her and got into her own bed.

After that, she lay awake until morning.

And that was to set the pattern of her nights from then on, for the next few days, for the next few weeks turning into months and then years. Every single night, she lay crammed into the bed with Maggie, sleeping fitfully, waking often with a start, turning to check that Lizzie was asleep.

She was not to know that Lizzie would neither forgive nor forget and that one day Nessa would pay the price dearly for borrowing the emerald green satin frock.

***

At eighteen, Nessa's head was still full of silly dreams but she kept quiet about them, avoiding taking a job in the weaving shed because she wanted something better. In the meantime, she cleaned over at a doctor's house in town, working hard and keeping her head down to avoid trouble. It aggravated her dad who accused her of having ideas above her station when most girls her age would be glad of the chance of a good steady job at the mill. Once you got in there, provided you kept your looms going and kept on the right side of the tackler, you had a job for as long as you wanted.

"Don't take any notice of him," her mother said on the quiet. "He thinks a job in the weaving shed is the best you can do and it isn't, love. I've heard tell there's a job going up in Market Place at that hair cutting saloon. They say there's a workroom at the back and they make umbrellas and walking sticks. If you can get in there you might learn a trade. Mind you, I've also heard tell that the boss is one for the ladies so you'll have to watch him."

Samuel Newsham with his sandy moustache and fancy waistcoat took one look at her and the job was hers. He put his hand on her waist as he escorted her into the workroom to show her what was being done, steadying her when she had no need of steadying, a firm hold with his big fat hand that instantly alerted her feminine senses. He was one to watch and no mistake but instinctively she knew she could handle him.

It wasn't much of a job. She was to make everybody cups of tea and keep the workroom and saloon clean and swept and tidy but, if a lady came in to get her hair done or to buy an umbrella or walking stick for her husband, she was to shut up and keep quiet.

She hated the way some of the ladies looked at her as if she was bit of muck stuck on their shoes. Some were nicer, giving her a sort of sympathetic smile as if they understood what her life was like although they couldn't begin to know the half of it.

She listened intently though, listened to the way they spoke, the way they acted because Mr Newsham flattered them something rotten, flattered even the plainest of ladies so that Nessa could see them simpering and smiling. Couldn't they see he didn't mean a word of it when she could see plain as the bulbous nose on his face? She had this knack of knowing what people were really thinking behind the look on their faces and she was rarely wrong.

In the workroom, she made the other girls laugh when she mimicked the way those ladies spoke because, even though she was not aware of it, she had a good ear.

"Nessa, come and sit up here," Mr Newsham said one evening, indicating the big chair in front of the mirror in the saloon. She was last in, having finished clearing up and he had taken off his barber's jacket and put the closed sign up.

She did as she was told, watching as he ran his fingers through her hair, hearing his breathing quicken and guessing that something was not quite right especially when his fingers strayed onto her neck and moved lightly up and down. She watched, her eyes on his, telling him without words what she was thinking. For two pins, she would flounce out here and now and tell him to stuff his job. But…

"You are a beautiful girl and you have lovely hair, Nessa," he said. "It has just the right amount of curl although it could do with a good trim."

"I'm not having an Eton crop. Nobody's going to do that to me," she said quickly in case he reached for the scissors.

"I'm not cutting your hair," he said with a short laugh. "I do the ladies' hair."

"My mum cuts mine when it needs doing," she told him. "She cuts all our hair, me, my sisters' and dad's. She even cuts Auntie Nelly's next door."

"Does she now? Quite a business going on." He seemed irritated and that pleased her even though she knew she was taking a chance in irritating him. She had learned though in the time she had been here that she could get away with a lot although she had also learned that there was a fine line between being impishly cheeky and really cheeky. One day she would step over the line and that would be that. "It's harder than it looks, cutting hair. It's not a job for amateurs. Now..." he let her hair fall heavily back into place, blessedly removing his fingers from her neck which still crawled from the effect as if a thousand insects had skittled across.

She put up her hand to rub at it but thankfully he was no longer looking directly at her.

"I've been thinking," he said. "You've been here a while now and I might let you start learning the trade in the workroom. Would you like that? It will be a bit more in your pay packet and you could stay behind now and then for me to explain things to you. It's a good trade and our walking sticks are well thought of."

Stay behind with him? What could she say?

***

"I might have to take a job in the weaving shed," she confided to Maggie. "I don't trust Mr Newsham. He flirts with everybody. And he has a wife and two children. I hope he doesn't think I'm flirting. I hate it, Maggie, when he touches me."

"You don't need to flirt. Men fall over themselves for girls like you. It's the curse of being pretty, our Nessa, and sometimes I am glad I'm just plain."

"Frank didn't think you were plain," Nessa told her gently, instantly sorry to have reminded her of her lost love.

"No but then we were two plain ones together," Maggie said. "But looks die so think on and stop all this nonsense dreaming about William Whitlock. I know you still think about him."

"How do you know that?" she asked and could have cut her tongue off for giving it away.

"I've seen you looking at his pictures in the paper and last week when we were in town he passed by us in his car, remember that, and I saw your face then. You blushed something rotten."

"No I did not. I was only looking at the car," she said quickly. "Big fancy thing."

Maggie smiled. "It's daft because it will get you nowhere, love. There are plenty of nice lads round here. Tony Walsh thinks a lot about you and you could do worse. He's got a job on the paper, love. He's a reporter now."

Tony was going places as he was keen to point out and she had grown to like him but did she like him enough? He made her laugh and he was not bad looking but he was also cleverer than most round here and she admired that. She knew that he liked her a lot although she was still holding him at arm's length, keeping it to kisses and just a little bit of touching but not down there. She wanted to keep herself proper for the man she would marry and she knew in her heart, saddened a little by that thought, that he wouldn't be Tony Walsh.

Nor would it be William Whitlock and she was a fool to think otherwise.

Forgetting him was easier said than done because, as Maggie pointed out, she caught sight of him from time to time out in his fancy car and sometimes there was his picture in the paper accompanied by that grim looking sister of his. As yet though, there was no sign of a lady in his life and, ridiculously, she clung onto that.

**

It was a long time before Nessa found out what a Medium was and she was both horrified and excited at the thought. That explained why, whenever Auntie Florence came into Peggy's corner shop, the chatter stopped instantly.

They all laughed about that, poking fun at her behind her back, but it was a scared sort of laughter and whenever she passed amongst them, they moved back a little to let her by, glancing nervously at her, at the way she glided about like a grey ghost.

And then, one by one, they drifted along to her séances.

After a long time, reluctantly but out of curiosity, her mother started to go along too. The séances or meetings as Auntie Florence called them were held at the Crawford's house and the reason her mother went along was simple. She wanted to speak to her brother Alf. She wanted to make sure he hadn't suffered to set her mind at rest and a lot of the other women needed to speak to their dead relatives too for the same reason.

"I shouldn't really be talking to you about it," her mum said. "I don't want to upset you, our Nessa and that's why I've tried to keep it quiet because young girls shouldn't know about such things. But you're old enough now and Maggie knows about it. We have to be careful we don't talk about it because the powers that be don't like it and we don't want to get Auntie Florence into any bother. They say it's witchcraft."

"Who do?"

"The powers that be, them higher ups at the Town Hall and even Mr Crawford himself, your Auntie Florence's husband, doesn't go along with it although he puts up with it. He's scared she'll be found out and he'll lose business hand over fist and that's why she doesn't talk about it when she's at those fancy dos at the Town Hall although I bet everybody knows." She sniffed. "You can't blow your nose round here without folks knowing. Anyway, there's a waiting list of folks wanting to go to the meetings because your Auntie Florence won't have more than six or seven there at a time. Too many folk and it spoils her concentration she says. Too many newcomers and it can be a wash-out so Hetty Parkinson says. Sometimes nowt happens. They all sit there and nowt happens and they get their money back although they still get a cup of tea and a biscuit." She shook her head in wonderment. "They get easily upset do the spirits."

Nessa laughed. "That's daft. I don't believe in it."

"Neither does your dad," her mother glanced round but he was outside in the yard. "He says it's meddling and we shouldn't do it so when I go I tell him I'm off to the pictures with Hetty and she says the same to her Billy. Don't breathe a word."

"I won't, Mum. What happens at these meetings?"

"Ssh." Her mother looked round as dad popped his head round the door and said he was off out. "All right, Harry love?"

He nodded. "What's for tea?"

"Hotpot and cabbage."

"Grand."

Once the door had closed behind him, she took hold of Nessa and drew her into the living room where they sat down.

"We sit in her front parlour," she said, eyes aglow with excitement mingled with a bit of fear. "She uses the front parlour because it's a little room which she says is perfect to contain the vibrations."

"Vibrations?" Nessa giggled, half alarmed too because her mother looked so serious.

"Yes."

"What are they?"

"I don't rightly know but I tell you, you can laugh all you like, Nessa, but I wish you wouldn't because it cheers folks up no end to get a message from the other side. It fair puts a bounce in their step if they hear good news from the other side."

"Do you have to pay her?" Nessa said, thinking of the practicalities and knowing her mum had to think about every last penny.

"She only charges a pittance but folks chip in a bit extra if they get a good message. Mind you, you pay a bit more for what she calls personal channelling. Some ladies come from up Fulwood or Penwortham, ladies with money and she does this personal channelling stuff for them."

"What is it?"

Her mother shook her head. "It means it's just you and her and them up there." She raised her eyes to the ceiling. "Private, like. It's for folks who don't like everybody listening in to their business."

"It's creepy. I don't like it."

"That's why I've not told you before. I don't want you upset and you won't be going along to a meeting either, not for a long time. She wouldn't let you anyway, not yet. She likes you does Auntie Florence." Her mother smiled. "I think it's because she has no babies herself and she wishes she did."

"Does Maggie…?" She thought about Maggie's Frank.

"No, she hasn't been because she doesn't believe in it and your Auntie Florence doesn't like to have folks there who don't believe because they upset the applecart. I think Maggie is frightened of getting a message from her Frank because she still thinks he's alive. We all know he's not," she added with a small smile. "But let her think what she wants if it makes it easier for her, poor love."

Despite herself, Nessa was intrigued by the whole business but scared at the same time and certainly in no hurry to be part of it.

"After it's over," her mother carried on. "We get a cup of tea and a biscuit and by God, love, we need it. My nerves are all a jangle until it's over."

"Have you had a message from Uncle Alf, mum?"

"Not yet. He'll be trying to get through but it's bedlam up there. It's like they are all trying to use one telephone, pushing and shoving each other – that's what your Auntie Florence says."

"But do you hear them, the other voices?"

"Never you mind." Her mother clammed up then and that was that.

***

Nessa had seen the Crawford's shop in Friargate although she had never been inside. Mr Herbert Crawford was a Silversmith and Watch Maker and the shop also had shelves of china and glassware so he was an important business man pictured in the paper sometimes with his wife at his side.

Once she realised what a Medium was, Nessa took a bit more notice of her although Maggie warned she should stay well away for Maggie was having no truck with all this other side business.

"Women like her are dangerous," she told Nessa. "And I've seen her looking at you. She's like a spider, one of those thin feathery ones, and you might get caught in her web."

Maggie hardly ever spoke like that, in such a fanciful way so Nessa took heed of it although for once she wasn't so sure that Maggie was right. When Maggie got a bee in her bonnet about somebody, she wouldn't shake it off.

Auntie Florence was tall and slender, in her mid-forties with the china-blue staring eyes of a doll. She was softly spoken which was odd in a district where the women were generally highly vocal and the women were in awe of her although as time went by they grew used to her and her ways. Grey must be her favourite colour because she often wore it and her clothes remained at nearly ankle-length when fashionable hemlines were wavering.

Things came to a head for Nessa one Friday evening. Her mother was having a rare night out at the music hall, Maggie had taken to her bed and Lizzie was nowhere to be found.

Her dad rolled home drunk and when he was drunk he turned nasty, lashing out at anybody and everybody. Tonight, Nessa was to bear the brunt.

"Lady…" he called out to her, swaying a little on his sturdy legs. "What's this I hear about you not going for the weaving job I told you about? Again. You could have had a dozen jobs at the mill if you'd bothered to go. It'll pay a damned sight more than that job at that shop. Who do you think you are, madam? My own daughter thinks she's too good for the weaving shed. Is that it?"

"No, dad," she said wearily. She might be sick of it, sick of Mr Newsham because it was getting worse but she still didn't want to go into the mill because she felt she would be trapped forever if she did. The promised promotion to learn the umbrella trade had yet to come to anything which was maybe a blessing but it still frustrated her.

"I'm a laughing stock," her dad yelled, coming towards her, eyes flashing with anger and pain. "I'll not have it. I've got one barmy daughter and I won't have another who thinks she's too big for her boots."

He swung at her, the blow catching her on the side of the head and sending her flying into the door post. He then staggered off, leaving her lying against the door, knocked out for a minute, tasting blood in her mouth when she came groggily to, her arm stinging because she had banged heavily into the door.

It had happened before and it would happen again but this time, as she got awkwardly to her feet, holding onto her arm, she felt she needed sympathy and, hardly aware of what she was doing and where she was going, she staggered out herself into the street, wiping her mouth, stumbling along before finding herself outside Auntie Florence's house.

She hammered on the door, incoherent by the time Auntie Florence opened it, forgetting all about the family promise to keep dad's outbursts private and blurting it out directly she was inside the house.

"Come on in. You look terrible," Auntie Florence steered her away from the parlour, that disturbing room, ushering her instead into the pretty sitting room with its cushions and flowery curtains. "I'll get some warm water to bathe your face. Are your teeth all right?"

She nodded, feeling inside her mouth with her tongue. Nothing loose.

"You sit yourself down, my dear, and then you can tell me all about it."

Nessa collapsed into the chair by the fireside, feeling all the strength going out of her. She steadied her breath, felt her heart returning to normal before Auntie Florence returned with a bowl and cloths.

"It's my dad." She knew she shouldn't be saying it but she said it anyway because she was fed up with it. "He was drunk and he knocked me into the door. Mum's out and our Maggie's bad and I didn't want to upset her and I don't know where Lizzie has got to. So, there was just me and him and he took his temper out on me. He's proper mad because I wouldn't go for the job at the mill. He's always telling me about jobs in the weaving shed."

"I thought as much," Auntie Florence said, tight lipped, when she had finished. "Your father has that look about him I'm afraid, a menacing look, and I hear that none of the mill-girls like working with him. He has this anger bubbling away inside of him and sometimes it erupts like a volcano People like him are dangerous and I fear your sister Lizzie has inherited it from him."

"I hate him when he's like that," Nessa said, sighing as Auntie Florence continued to gently bathe her face, wincing as she touched her eye. "I hate him and I know it's a sin to say it but I do. He doesn't love me or any of us, not even Mum but she never sticks up for us, always takes his side whatever he does."

"She's a kind woman but she's easily led, poor soul, and she loves him or she thinks she does," Auntie Florence said, patting her face dry with a soft clean towel. "Why don't you have a good cry? A good cry does you good."

"I can't. I never can after I've had a walloping," she said with a sniff.

Auntie Florence put her arm round her and, for a moment, she leaned into her, breathing in a flowery scent, but still she didn't cry even though the sympathy was almost unbearable as Auntie Florence gently stroked her hair and whispered soothing noises.

"I wish you were my mum," she said at last.

"No you don't. Please don't say that. Olive is a good mum. She does her very best for you all. She feeds you well and she keeps the house clean and tidy."

"Yes but you would stand up to him, wouldn't you? He would be frightened of you. He's frightened of ghost stuff so he would be scared of you."

"Listen, Vanessa, I have an idea." Auntie Florence sat down in the chair -opposite. "I've been thinking about something for a very long time and now seems a good moment to start talking about it."

"What do you mean?"

"Your mother tells me that you are having some trouble at work with that barber gentleman. Has he been making advances?"

"Oh him…" Nessa cringed as she moved, her shoulder sore from its brush with the door frame. "His hands wander but I can handle him and I'm not going to work in the mill no matter what my dad says."

"No, you are not. You can do much better than that, a girl with your looks," Auntie Florence told her. "You have to learn to use your looks and I know how you can do that. I need you to be patient for a little longer but I am going to help you. I have an idea that concerns both of us."

"What is it?" Nessa frowned, remembering Maggie's warnings about this lady. "It's nothing to do with…" she gestured towards the parlour. "I'm having nowt to do with ghosts and stuff."

Auntie Florence laughed. "It's nothing to do with them although ghosts are nothing to be afraid of. I want to know first of all if you trust me."

She nodded.

"You've had a shock. You need to rest a while. You must stay with me for a few days."

"I can't. I have to go to work tomorrow."

"No, you cannot. You will have some dreadful bruises by tomorrow and probably a black eye too. Your barber gentleman will not like that as it may reflect on him so I will send a message to him and to your mother so she does not worry."

And that is what happened and for the next week Nessa was cared for in a way she had never been cared for before. Her mother and Maggie popped round to see her, saying they hadn't told dad where she was and, of course, they had kept it from Lizzie too.

"I've spoken to him," her mum told her, eyes full of grief. "He's not himself when he's drunk and he can't remember anything. He's very sorry if he hurt you, love. We have to keep him away from the booze because he's not like that, not when he's sober. He's a good man when he's sober and he thinks the world of us."

"You shouldn't allow it, Olive," Auntie Florence dared to say but her mother gave her short shrift for daring to say it, threatening to remove Nessa there and then but relenting when Nessa pleaded to be allowed to stay a while longer.

Over that week, pampered as she was, Nessa's aches gradually eased and she spent her time reading because it turned out Auntie Florence subscribed to the Book-Lovers Library run by Boots the Chemist. Nessa wallowed in the stories. She was a good reader as she had picked reading up quickly at the rough school she had attended. The only book they had in their house was what

Dad called the good book, the Bible and Nessa couldn't make head or tail of that.

Auntie Florence also had copies of Picturegoer lurking around and Nessa lapped those up because she loved to keep up with what was happening in the glamorous world in America.

To go there was yet another of her silly dreams. Nessa knew in her heart her dreams were impossible, like trying to catch a whisper or weave a dress from the mist but she could still dream, couldn't she?

"Would you like to go to America, mum?" she had asked, thinking of her mother's friend who had done just that. "If you were on your own like Cissie Parker?"

"No, I would not. And anyway, I'm not on my own, am I, love? And I hope I never am because I wouldn't be able to live without your dad. I know he lets rip sometimes…" she gave a deep heartfelt sigh. "But he's a grand man and everything he does, he does for us. Being a tackler is a gradely job and he's worked hard for it and we all need him to look after us. I tell you, if anything happens to him, I won't last five minutes on my own."

Years later, Nessa was to recall those words with a shiver.

CHAPTER THREE

"Your mum's had a turn, Nessa," her dad said, catching Nessa as she got in from work. "I can't make her out so get in there and see if you can make any sense of it. It must be woman's stuff," he added, cheeks flushing. "Our Maggie's seeing to the tea."

Nessa went into the front room where her mother was sitting, eyes glazed over, absentmindedly wringing her hands. As Nessa approached, kneeling beside her, she moved her head and smiled a little. She was looking so much older these days, old and tired.

"What is it, Mum? What's up?"

Her mother put a finger up to her lips and leaned forward, whispering. "I went to a meeting at your Auntie Florence's this afternoon and he finally got a message through to me."

"Uncle Alf?" she caught her mother's excitement. "What did he say?"

"He said it was all right, the passing over, quick and he didn't feel that much. He asked after you although you were only a babe when he last saw you." Her eyes filled with tears. "He was only a young man, a lovely young man and he had all his life in front of him but he seemed all right. Cheerful even."

"That's good then." She took hold of her mother's clammy hand. She didn't know what to believe, whether or not there had really been a message or whether it was some sort of trick. If it was a trick, it was awful and she understood just why Maggie was so suspicious of Auntie Florence. She had asked a lot of questions about her after the week Nessa spent with her. It had made Nessa wonder if Maggie was not just a little bit jealous of the way Auntie Florence was worming her way into Nessa's life – at least that was how Maggie saw it and she did not like it one little bit.

"It gave me a shock, love, knocked me for six to hear his voice. He sounded funny but that's the vibrations," her mum went on, trembling a little and holding fast onto Nessa's hand. "And that's not all. Frank sent a message too for Maggie but I don't know whether to tell her because…" she bit her lip. "You know she thinks he might be alive somewhere trying to find his way home to her and that's what keeps her going. Without that hope, she would just fade away and I don't want that. I don't want to lose her just yet although I know I will lose her one day." Her eyes filled with tears and she shuddered at that thought.

"Don't tell her," Nessa said. "There's no need. We'll keep it quiet." She glanced round. "Where's Lizzie? She's not in, is she?"

"No. Don't tell her either."

"As if I would."

"Thanks, love." She sighed and scrambled up. "Best get tea started."

"Maggie's seeing to it. Shall I tell him you're feeling better now?"

She nodded, smiling thinly.

"He must never know," she said. "Never. If he finds out what I've been doing behind his back, I dread to think what will happen."

***

After that week spent there, Nessa often stopped off at Auntie Florence's house, usually without telling Maggie, and one autumn evening as they were having a cup of tea in the sitting room, Auntie Florence finally got round to saying what must have been on her mind for a very long time.

It was a cold miserable day and Nessa was feeling miserable too because things at work were going from bad to worse. There was a new barber assistant, a thin long streak of a man with limbs so loose he looked like a string puppet and he had touched her breast this afternoon, supposedly accidentally.

With a deep sigh, she accepted a piece of cake from the plate Auntie Florence offered her and, before that lady could ask what was the matter, she changed the subject to the one thing that she loved; the pictures and the film stars.

"Do film stars really love each other when they kiss in the picture?" she asked, balancing the china plate on her knee trying not to drop crumbs as Auntie Florence sat opposite, the folds of her grey skirt almost down to the floor, black shoes just peeping out.

"They act, my dear. Pretend. No, I don't believe they do love each other. Often, in real life, they are married to somebody else."

She nodded. She had known that already but it was such a shame because it looked as if they did love each other, the heroine's eyes shining as she listened to the lovely words the hero uttered.

"What's the matter?" Auntie Florence asked gently. "You seem subdued. Is it work?"

"It's the new barber," she admitted for it was a waste of time trying to hide things from this lady. "He's going to be every bit as bad as Mr

Newsham. He's already had one girl in tears but I shan't cry. None of them will see me cry."

"You have such bad luck with men, my dear. Believe me, they are not all like that. There are some good men around."

"I know," she said, a vision of William Whitlock appearing in her head because she just knew he would be kind and loving to the lucky woman he chose to marry. "But I might have to leave the shop, Auntie Florence. I can manage Mr Newsham but if there are two of them..." she left the words unsaid. "I might have to take a job in the mill," she added wearily, knowing when she was beaten.

"Vanessa..." Auntie Florence put down her plate and became suddenly crisp as she sat up straight. "I have something to ask you. Would you like to come with me to London?"

"London?" She had heard about it, bits on the wireless, read about it but it was just a distant place so far away and inaccessible it might as well have been the moon. "For a visit?"

"No."

"To live there, you mean?"

Auntie Florence nodded. "I'll have a word with your mother. You're not yet twenty one so we should tell her and your father what we intend to do. I don't want to go behind their backs."

"No." Nessa said at once, "Don't tell her. She'll say no and you mustn't tell Dad. He'll go crackers and knock me to kingdom come."

"Olive won't mind if she knows you are coming with me. She knows I will look after you. I'll see you come to no harm."

"She will mind," Nessa said, thinking of the money she handed over every week and the pocket money she got back. "Please don't tell them, Auntie Florence."

"Then you do want to come with me?"

"Yes but I don't see how I can. Where will we live?"

"I was born in London and I have a house there. It belonged to my parents and a cousin of mine has been living in it whilst I've been up here. Mr Crawford does not know about it," she explained, lowering her voice although that gentleman was at the shop in town. "My cousin died recently and I have to decide what to do about the house. I have money, my dear, a private allowance that Mr Crawford is not aware of and that is most adequate for my needs. I am more than capable of looking after myself."

"Are you?"

She nodded. "My business is lucrative too. Some of the ladies like to reward me with a bit extra and indeed one of my wealthier clients recently left me something in her will. She was so pleased, you see, to get in touch with her son and it made her own passing so much easier. My clients need to know if their loved ones suffered, to know they are all right. It gives them great comfort."

"What if they did suffer?"

Auntie Florence looked at her with her staring blue eyes and frowned.

"What if they suffered?" Nessa repeated. "Do they tell you? Do you tell their mums and their sweethearts if they did?"

"If there is suffering, it is blessedly brief and the passing over itself is always peaceful. There are spirits who are commissioned to help ease the passing," Auntie Florence said, looking at her closely. "I've spoken to the dead often enough not to be worried about dying. And don't you worry about it either. There is nothing to be afraid of."

There was a moment's silence as Nessa tried to make sense of it. She knew that Maggie, placid a woman as they come, would tear into Auntie Florence if she heard her speaking about such matters, mumbo jumbo she called it. She could almost hear Maggie's voice warning her again and again to step away and to have nothing to do with her. It was wicked stuff and Auntie Florence had no business filling silly women's heads with such daft ideas, according to Maggie that is.

But Maggie was destined to stay here forever, waiting for the man who would never come back and here was Nessa's chance to get away, to escape.

"What will I do in London?" she asked finally. "Will I get a job?"

"You can help me in the house and help with the séances. Help me get them organised. Send out the invitations. Take the money discreetly afterwards, organise repeat sessions for those who wish to partake of private channelling. I try to encourage that. Everything, you understand, has to be done carefully for there are always people trying to cause trouble, to cast seeds of doubt, to accuse people like me of wrongdoing, those who do not believe." She looked closely at her. "You do believe, don't you?"

"Well…" she spluttered. "I don't know. It doesn't seem right getting in touch with dead folk."

Auntie Florence smiled a little. "I understand your doubts and I don't blame you for having them. Those who doubt require a rational explanation for what goes on and they try to prove séances are faked but they cannot prove mine fake because they are not. I know that some people try to catch me out and, because the spirits do not like hostile vibrations, I refuse to let them come if I feel uneasy about their motives, which of course makes them all the more convinced I have something to hide."

Nessa listened, shivering as the room grew cold, the fire going out and Auntie Florence's calm voice droning on.

"I see you have doubts so let me explain. How could it be done?" she asked Nessa. "To have a satisfactory outcome, I would have to employ actors and actresses, a great number, to adequately cover the spirits known to the people at my séance. As I can never be completely sure who will attend, my actors would have to be on stand-by, lines rehearsed for any situation that may arise. They would also have to have an intimate knowledge of the people in the room. Twenty or more voices may speak at one séance and sometimes it resembles a very excited party gathering. They can be very chatty on the other side, interrupting each other and so on. It's far more disorganised than here."

Nessa tried to picture it but because she had never attended a séance, that was hard.

"No two sittings are the same," Auntie Florence continued, playing now with the string of pearls at her neck. "There are always new spirits coming through and, as the sittings take place in the dark there must be no fumbling or hesitation amongst the actors, no opportunity to check their lines, no rustling of paper. And where would they all hide? Behind a curtain? And all this going on, all these comings and goings of actors without anybody seeing them arrive. And the cost… think about the cost of employing these brilliant actors. Tell me now, how do I fake it?"

"I don't know," she whispered. "I don't know."

"Some evenings are disappointing," she went on. "You know when you listen to the wireless and you lose the station and have to twiddle the knobs?"

She nodded. They had a terrible wireless set at home and it was always humming and going off and nobody but dad was allowed to twiddle the knobs and fiddle with it making it ten times worse because he did not have a gentle touch.

"They are easily upset, the spirits," Auntie Florence said, echoing what her mother had told her. "We sit in the same places and we touch fingers and close our eyes because in order to receive them you must have an open and relaxed mind and a receptive heart. Now…" she smiled and sat up straighter. "Does that satisfy you, my dear?"

"I suppose so," she said reluctantly.

"And you will make the tea afterwards because they always want a good strong cup of tea when it's over. If you come with me to London, I will pay you, more than you would get in the mill or the shop and I will provide you with food and lodging but you are not to tell anybody of this, not until it's settled. I am leaving Mr Crawford and you are to be ready to leave for London next week."

"Next week? But..." she was struggling to comprehend this. She did not know Mr Herbert Crawford very well but he had always seemed courteous and respectful, never having laid a finger on her. "Why are you leaving him?" she asked, looking round anxiously as if he should suddenly appear.

"That is private, my dear."

"Sorry." She muttered, feeling her cheeks flame.

"When you are older, you will understand why. Some marriages are made in heaven but I regret that mine was not. I shall be quite happy living the rest of my life without a man in attendance."

Nessa still did not understand but she was wise enough to know not to probe too much. She would understand if her mother left her father although that would never happen but Mr Crawford seemed a nice gentleman. For a moment, the silence reigned, uncomfortable now and then Auntie Florence began to speak again.

"You are such a beauty, Vanessa, and you are wasted here. If you stay, you will be ground to bits like the rest of them. You will get married to some local boy like Tony Walsh…"

So she knew about that. Mrs Crawford seemed to know everything.

"The children will come along quickly," she continued. "And that will be that. If you come with me to London, I shall not come back and nor will you."

"Do you really hear voices?" she asked, her mind made up. She was risking it. She was going to London come what may. "Voices from the dead?" she persisted as Auntie Florence seemed disinclined to answer.

"I thought I had explained fully," she said, exasperated now. "You must not doubt that. If you do doubt then I cannot take you with me. My conscience is clear. Faint they are sometimes but that is because of the trouble they have with the vibrations. That is why they sound strange. It is a gift, Vanessa, and I did not ask for it. All I do is pass on the messages. That is really all there is to it. I cannot ignore my gift and people get comfort and consolation from it."

Nessa nodded, convincing herself or at least half convincing herself. In any case, anything was better than working in an umbrella workshop and forever dodging the unwelcome attention of those two men.

She was going to London.

***

"London? I might have known. I wish I was coming with you," Maggie said.

"Why don't you? Auntie Florence won't mind. She has lots of money, she said so. I'll ask her, Maggie."

"No. She hasn't asked me, she's asked you. Anyway, I can't leave Mum with him. He's going to go daft when you leave. And then there's Lizzie."

Yes. There was Lizzie and Nessa felt badly about leaving Maggie to cope with her. Lizzie never changed, never got any better. She was still working at the house in Ashton, still washing up, still spending her days grumbling, eyes flashing, and still wearing the bangle.

"I suppose I could ask Auntie Florence if she could come too," she said doubtfully. "She can always help clean up. And you shouldn't worry about Mum, Maggie. Dad won't harm her and it might be better for her if we leave the two of them alone to look after each other."

"Don't be daft." Maggie half smiled. "I've told you that Auntie Florence likes pretty things round her. She has no time for the likes of me or Lizzie. Haven't you noticed? In any case, Lizzie won't leave Preston. She's too scared to leave Preston."

"I'm scared to leave Preston," Nessa admitted and it was true. It was frightening to leave all that was familiar, all you had ever known, the same old sights and sounds but she had to take the chance. If she didn't then she would wonder forever what it would have been like. "But I feel bad about leaving you here, Maggie."

"Don't. I have to stay. Suppose my Frank comes home." Maggie managed a sad smile. "He's only missing, presumed dead so they have never found him and he won't know where I am, will he, if I've gone from here."

"But Frank…" She very nearly blurted it out, blurted out that Mum had had a message from him but she could not do it. She could not destroy that tiny bit of hope in her sister's eyes. Sometimes she wondered if losing Frank had sent Maggie a little mad for she talked of the War as if it was yesterday when it was years past. "Auntie Florence says we can write letters to each other," she went on. "She will send my letters to a friend of hers,

Mrs Flintoff and she will pass them on to the corner shop and you can pick them up from there and give Peggy at the shop your letters to me then she will pass them on to Mrs Flintoff because nobody must know our address in London. Auntie Florence doesn't want Mr Crawford to know and she doesn't want anybody coming down to bring me back either."

Maggie frowned. She could write in a nice hand and read much better than their mum who struggled with it. "It seems a right old palaver," Maggie said with a sniff. "All this secret stuff and who's to know this Mrs Flintoff will do what she says. And who's to say that Peggy at the shop won't blab."

"She's being paid. We have to trust the two of them."

"It's not just them we have to trust. We have to trust her too," Maggie huffed but that was the plan and they would stick to it.

***

Coming out of the room after her chat with Maggie, she nearly fell over Lizzie who had been listening at the door.

"London Bridge is falling down, falling down …" she chanted, low. "Where's she going then? Where's our Nessa going tomorrow?"

"Oh Lizzie, shush…" she looked round anxiously. "You're not to tell mum or dad. Please don't spoil things for me."

Lizzie rubbed at the bangle which she wore at all times, even in bed, even when she plunged her hands into scummy washing up water. Considering it was cheap metal, it was looking good still.

"You and your fancy ideas," Lizzie seethed, eyes wild. "Just because you're pretty, our Nessa, you think you can have anything you want. Well, you can't. You can't have that William Whitlock for a start." Lizzie, even though she was small, had a knack of making the most of her size and blocked her way, jamming her against the wall of the narrow landing. "And if you better yourself, you'll not want to be bothered with the likes of us again, will you? I'm your sister, blood to blood, and don't forget that."

"I won't," Nessa tried a smile, looking at Lizzie whose protruding eyes seemed to protrude even further when she was angry. "I'll send you money when I have money. I'll get it to you somehow."

"Don't want your money. I wouldn't come to London if you begged me," Lizzie said. "And it's not because I'm frightened of leaving Preston either, no matter what Maggie says."

"Promise me you won't tell," Nessa said. "If you do then it's over between us. I'll never speak to you again, Lizzie Cookson, and I'll have that bangle back."

Lizzie clutched it then, staring at her, before giving a quick nod. "All right. I won't tell. Just remember what I've done for you, our Nessa. You're all right, you are, better than Maggie because all she can think about is her Frank who's dead in a trench somewhere, rotted away by now."

"Don't you dare say that to Maggie."

"She doesn't need telling. She knows. So, you are leaving us then?"

"I have to, Lizzie. I'm scared but I have to see what's what down there in London."

Lizzie nodded, staring at her. "I remember the day you were born. She had a right old time with you, did Mum. Screamed the house down. I thought she was a goner and then there you were, the littlest thing I have ever seen. When you were a baby, mum wouldn't let me hold you in case I dropped you. I wanted to hold you." For a moment, there was a trace of tears in her eyes which was a shock because Lizzie never cried. "Mum never lets me hold the babies round here. I never get to hold them and I would be ever so careful with them. I love babies."

"I know you do." Nessa smiled, suddenly feeling a great sadness for this little scrap of a woman. "I'll let you hold my baby one day."

"Will you? Promise."

"Cross my heart and hope to die."

Lizzie gave a rare smile, changing her face completely, giving a hint of what she might look like if she made an effort.

"I might miss you a bit," she admitted. "I don't know for sure but I might."

Nessa could not sleep that night for excitement knowing it would be the last time she would sleep beside Maggie in this bed. She lay awake, staring at the ceiling and thinking of her new life. She was giving up on William Whitlock by moving away but she was grown up enough to know that all that had been a silly young girl's dream.

***

Next day, after a final furtive and tearful goodbye to Maggie, carrying just a few items precious to her, she set off just after dawn to meet up with Auntie Florence. She left a note with Maggie for her mum that Maggie would help her to read telling her not to worry and that she would see her again soon – a lie, but a necessary one.

There was a chill in the morning air as she hurried to the meeting place at the top end of Marsh Lane, glad that there was no-one around for her footsteps seemed loud on the rough pavement. As she neared the end of the road, taking to the back alley, she heard a lavatory flush and a yard door opened and, although she nearly ran past, a voice called out to her.

"Nessa! Where are you off to?"

She spun round. It was Tony Walsh, tucking his shirt into his trousers and pulling up his braces. He was fair haired with a ruddy complexion, big and burly, a good looking young man and she knew that other girls envied her because she was the one who had won his heart.

"Tony." She stopped as he came towards her, a puzzled look on his face.

"What are you doing up and about at this time? Are you running away?" he asked with a grin, that lopsided smile she knew well. Over this last year they had spent more than enough time in the back row of the picture house together and been to a few dances at Columba Dance Hall. They were starting to be seen as a couple and it wouldn't be long before he would have to make a move and go and see her dad before folks started to talk and before too long she knew she would be walking up the aisle towards him. He had been patient with her but she knew he was becoming exasperated with her for holding him off as she did.

"What are you doing, Nessa Cookson, in your best coat and hat?" he persisted, eyes merry as he looked at her.

"Never you mind, Tony." She tugged at the belt of her coat and put a hand up to her blue felt cloche hat, feeling cornered and not knowing what to say.

"You are running away, aren't you?" he said as the truth dawned, his eyes instantly losing their sparkle. "You can't do that, Nessa."

"I can and I am," she said, "Don't try to stop me."

"But why? You can't leave me. I thought that you and me … I love you."

"It's the first time you've told me that," she said, looking towards the end of the street where Auntie Florence would even now be waiting in the car. It was a shock to hear those words, the first time a man had ever said those words to her but it was wrong. It was not like this in the pictures. The hero did not tell the heroine he loved her for the first time in a grubby cobbled back alley on a cold grey morning with him in his shirt and braces, rough shaven and sleepy eyed.

"I'll talk to your father and we'll start walking out proper," he told her, searching her face for a reaction. "You do love me, don't you?" He reached for her and drew her close and she could smell the morning man-smell of him, feel the sturdiness of his shoulder, for a moment aching to be held close in those strong arms.

"Let me go, Tony." She broke free and he made no attempt to draw her back. "I've got to go. I've got to try it."

They stood, together, in the dingy alley as the cold morning sun struggled to break through the heavy clouds and a few spits of rain began.

After a long moment, he nodded. "Go then." His voice changed, tightened as did his face.

"She's waiting for me. Auntie Florence," she said, not knowing why she was telling him that. "Maggie knows about it."

"Give me your address," he said urgently. "Tell me. I'll remember it."

She shook her head. "I don't know. She hasn't told me."

"Be careful, Nessa." He suddenly looked quite wretched standing there. "She's a funny one with all that dangerous talk of hers. It isn't right, trying to talk to the dead."

Swiftly, she reached up and kissed him one last time, choked as she muttered goodbye, before turning and running the last bit. The decision, right or wrong, was made and her mind was spinning because, although she wasn't sure if she really loved Tony, he seemed to love her and maybe that was enough. Maybe…

She looked back but the alley was now empty and she paused at the top, shaken by what had just happened. Then, picking up her bag, tugging at the belt of her coat, she turned the corner to where she could see the car, starting to run as the rain began in earnest.

"You are late," Auntie Florence rebuked her as she climbed in "Drive on," she instructed the driver. "I knew you would do it, Vanessa," she went on as they set off, reaching for her hand and giving it an encouraging squeeze. "It can't have been easy but you have courage, my dear. You will love the house in London and, as soon as we are settled, you must sit in at one of the séances. Isn't that exciting?"

Exciting and terrifying at the same time.

If she could have leapt out of the car at that moment and run back to Tony she would have but it was too late for they were speeding on their way.

CHAPTER FOUR

London

The London house was in the middle of a terrace like the one she had been born in but there were trees in this street with smart black railings either side of the steps leading to the front door.

"Come on in," Auntie Florence said, unpinning her hat and looking round with pleasure. Nessa followed her gaze, her eyes drawn to the ceiling with its cream cornice of sunflowers. Nessa was to have a bedroom to herself with flowery pink wallpaper, and there was a bathroom with a proper bath. It was all so different from bathing in the old tin bath at home, the water cool and scummy by the time it was her turn.

Later, Auntie Florence explained that, now they were here, things would change. Firstly, she was to stop calling her Auntie Florence but refer to her instead as Mrs Crawford and secondly, she was to make no mention of life in Preston. Mrs Crawford wished to dissociate herself from that place and so must she.

"As to your name, my dear, you will be known as Vanessa," Mrs Crawford went on. "Why on earth did your mother call your sisters Margaret and Elizabeth and then shorten them to Maggie and Lizzie?"

"I like the name Maggie," she said. "And Lizzie has always been just Lizzie."

"I agree. She looks like a Lizzie," Mrs Crawford said with a shudder. "You must forget them both."

"But I am going to write to Maggie, aren't I?" Nessa said. "Mrs Flintoff will pass letters on to her, won't she? You said that Peggy at the shop would keep hold of them and see Maggie gets them."

"For a while perhaps but eventually it will end. Time apart will bring it to a close. You must forget your past life." She smiled serenely. "The first thing is to lose that dreadful accent. I knew as soon as we got you away from there, you would blossom. All we must think about now is the future. Your future, Vanessa."

Forget the past. Nessa felt a moment's panic. How could she do that?

"Don't look so worried, my dear. We are going to take the time to learn how to speak properly, how to act in society so that in good time you will be accepted as of right. You are a quick learner and it won't take long. You stood out amongst the

63

rest, Vanessa, and I saw it from the beginning. I will always be at your side for a while whenever we meet people. I shall be there guiding you, protecting you, and it's surprising how you can get by simply smiling and saying the odd word. In fact, it will be perfectly appropriate for you to appear quiet and shy. I will school you."

The prospect sounded terrifying but she was reminded of the barber's shop and how she had mimicked the ladies' way of talking and made the other girls laugh.

"Why are you doing this for me, Auntie Florence?"

"Mrs Crawford, dear, and surely you know the answer to that. I was never blessed with children," she said. "And you are the daughter I would have liked to have; a bright girl with backbone. I saw that in you from the beginning. It would have been a sin to leave you behind. I have plans for you and I intend that you shall marry a man of means."

She knew what that meant. Somebody such as William Whitlock for he was a man of means but sadly it would not be him. Auntie Florence might mean a portly older gentleman rather like Mr Crawford and her heart sank at that thought.

"I have invented a suitable background for you. We will change your name. You will be Vanessa

Jones from the Welsh borders, a distant relative of mine. Your father George was a country solicitor, your dearest mama Priscilla an invalid. Here..." Mrs Crawford reached for her handbag and produced a rather tatty well-thumbed photograph which Nessa – Vanessa – was to keep in her bag. It showed a man and woman and a little girl with dark curly hair.

Vanessa liked the look of them and she particularly loved the frilly dress the girl was wearing and the ribbon in her hair forgetting for a moment that it was not actually her. The father in the photograph must be a good man and her well-read invalid mother must have been sweet and kind. By the time she came to live with Mrs Crawford, they were of course both conveniently dead. She was to be vague if asked about them, saying it upset her to talk of them and that would forestall any further questions.

"Vanessa Jones..." she repeated the name softly.

"Have no doubt we can do this, Vanessa, and with my help you will become a young lady and one day you will marry well."

"I'm only marrying for love," she reminded her for they had often talked of that. "I'm not marrying just anybody even if he does have money. I don't care about that. I have to love him first and he has to love me too."

"We all want to be loved but the important thing is to marry a man who will care for you, a man who will be proud that you are his wife. Love, my dear, the romantic kind you dream of, the kind you see in your films, is a complete nonsense. Adaptability and compromise is the key to a happy marriage."

Vanessa could not help a little huff of disbelief for who was she to talk, her own marriage being hardly the stuff of dreams.

Mrs Crawford gave her a sharp look as if she had spoken aloud. "It has been on my mind for years of how I could rescue you, my dear, from such a pitiful existence, from such inadequate parents, from such mean sisters …"

"Maggie isn't mean," Nessa said at once. "Lizzie is a bit but Maggie is good. Maggie…"

Mrs Crawford held up her hand and shushed her. "No more talk of Maggie. Now I think we will retire. It has been a long day and we are both very tired."

It took a long time to drift off to sleep that first night in the house in London but at last she did, dreaming of her home up in Lancashire, dreaming of Maggie, dreaming agitatedly of her father who would skin her alive if he ever caught up with her, and dreaming fleetingly – as she so often did – of the man she thought of as her knight in shining armour; William Whitlock.

***

Weeks later and it was her first séance. She had spent the previous weeks listening to the radio, hearing those lovely voices, mimicking them but now, the day of the séance, would she be hearing other voices?

The six guests arrived and Vanessa was introduced but, as per her instructions, said little, accepting condolences at the loss of her parents with a grateful smile.

With Mrs Crawford's guidance, she had helped prepare the parlour. The large circular table was ready, the red cloth spread on it, the chairs arranged at precise intervals around it.

As the clock struck eight, Mrs Crawford clapped her hands for attention.

"If we are all ready, ladies and gentlemen," she said. "Perhaps we might go through to the parlour."

Deceptively casual although Vanessa could detect the nervous excitement, they drifted out leaving her to bring up the rear. She followed the last person in and closed the door, wishing all the while she had the courage to run away before it was too late.

The lights were already dimmed.

Just one candle flickered, casting shadows. They sat down and Mrs Crawford began to speak.

"May I remind you to keep as still as you can and do not cross your legs," she said, her face pale in the dim light. "Hold hands with the person next to you so we have an unbroken circle. For the two newcomers this evening, Miss Earnshaw and my dear charge, Vanessa, try to stay calm. Remember they want to reach us and they do us no harm. Think of them sitting around, waiting to speak to us. If it's any consolation, I think they are just as anxious as we are."

They opened the sitting with a hymn to help the vibrations along as Mrs Crawford had previously explained to her. The hymn was "Guide Me O Thou Great Redeemer" followed by the Lord's Prayer. Terrified now, Vanessa was still, startled as another voice, a wavering one, joined in the Amen.

Her arms tingled with a sudden surge of energy running down to her fingertips and thence to the people on either side, both experienced sitters, who had smiled encouragingly at her before they began.

"We ask that the spirits join with us tonight," Mrs Crawford said, her voice stronger and more authoritative than normal.

The silence following her words lengthened.

The clock ticked.

The candle went out.

Now she could smell roses when there were none and the room grew colder. She gasped and the person on her right squeezed her hand.

"I don't think…" Mrs Crawford said and then a new reedy voice suddenly piped up.

"Good evening. I bring you news of a young man, a seafaring man called James. He has just come over and has had to leave behind his fiancée. I have a message for Doris Earnshaw."

"I am Doris." A timid voice from across the table.

"He apologises that he is unable to give the message himself but having just come across, he is not yet accomplished enough so the message comes through me. He says he was carried over very gently from the sea and felt no pain but he is sorry to leave you behind, Doris. You have much time before you join him but rest assured he will be waiting with open arms to receive you when the time comes. He asks if you remember seeing The Jazz Singer   and what happened afterwards?

Goodnight, dearest one, he says, and sweet dreams."

The lady was weeping.

The messages came through thick and fast, so many that Vanessa lost track, recalling what Mrs Crawford had said about actors. Where were the voices coming from if not from the other side?

When the voices faltered, they sang The Lord is My Shepherd to revive them but it was not to be for they were gone.

The sitting ended with a prayer and a moment's reflection before the lights came on and they stared, blinking, at each other. Standing up, for a minute she felt dizzy but managed to find her legs again making her way with the others from the room. She recalled her mother's words, her alarm when she heard from her brother Alf, and she now understood.

"I was frightened but I am so glad I came, Vanessa," Doris Earnshaw caught hold of her arm, eyes shining. She was a very pretty young woman, not much older than Vanessa, her eyes still a little blurry from her tears. "You don't know how wonderful it was to get a message from James. And only he knows about The Jazz Singer and what happened afterwards." She blushed and Vanessa could have hugged her, so pleased for her, but this lady was a mere acquaintance and such a gesture would have been inappropriate.

***

Vanessa woke, one bitterly cold morning, pulling the blankets closer to her and savouring the warmth. She felt just a little sick but that might have been the effects of the chocolate she had consumed late last night. Mrs Crawford had a sweet tooth and sometimes bought them a little treat, a Fry's Turkish Delight for herself and a Bournville chocolate bar for Vanessa but, next time, she vowed she would not eat it all in one go.

"Vanessa…" Mrs Crawford rapped on the door and peeped round. "Good morning, my dear. I've brought you a cup of tea."

She struggled to a sitting position, puzzled because it was her job to bring a cup up to Mrs Crawford but this morning, that lady was up and dressed already and, after handing her the cup, she sat down in the chair by the window.

"It's frosty out," she said, shivering although the air in the room was not completely chill even if the fire in the grate had long ago extinguished.

Vanessa reached for her bed-jacket and slipped it on before taking a welcome sip of tea.

"We shall need to wrap up warmly later," Mrs Crawford said. She was wearing a velveteen jacket in deep purple over one of her grey woollen dresses. "I have had a letter from my dearest friend Mrs Flintoff." she said, her manner awkward.

"Oh. Is she well?" she asked. She was never to appear too eager to learn of the contents of the letters for Mrs Flintoff always mentioned Maggie and sometimes Lizzie and Mrs Crawford often looked quite pained to be even discussing such matters. Clearly, she hoped Vanessa would soon decide to put an end to the correspondence but Vanessa persisted whilst there was a chance that Maggie got to read hers. As yet though, there had been no reply, no letter written in Maggie's hand just mentions of her and the rest of them in Mrs Flintoff's letters.

"Mrs Flintoff is tolerably well although her son is leading her a merry dance. I don't like to say as much but Arthur is something of a cad, I'm afraid."

"I'm sorry," Vanessa said politely.

"However, I have news to impart."

She shifted in the bed, suddenly alarmed at Mrs Crawford's expression. "I am so sorry to tell you, Vanessa, that your sister Maggie is gravely ill."

"I must go up to her." Agitated, she put her cup down and swung her legs out of bed, the skirt of her nightgown riding up so high that Mrs Crawford quickly averted her eyes.

"No, no. Oh dear me, you misunderstand," she said in dismay. "What I mean, what I should have said, is she has passed over, my dear. From all accounts, it started as another chest infection and then turned to pneumonia. She was taken to the Infirmary but it was all over within the week."

"Passed over? Sitting on the edge of the bed, Vanessa stilled, her limbs heavy. Maggie had never been strong but always pulled through her bad dos. "Do you mean she's dead?"

Mrs Crawford came across to sit on the bed and, at once Vanessa leaned close to her, the shock making her dizzy. The jacket was soft to lean against and smelled comfortingly of Eau de Cologne.

"Cry for Maggie, if you want, Nessa," Mrs Crawford's voice came from afar. "But I am afraid you cannot go home for the funeral."

Startled by the use of her old name, she nodded, remembering a younger Maggie picking her up and holding her close like this. She remembered leaving her that morning when she came to London. She nearly changed her mind, would have, but Maggie gave her a little forward push and then turned her back on her.

That was the very last time she saw her.

It was too late to go back home. Mrs Crawford was right. She would have to do her mourning at a distance.

"Come down for breakfast when you're ready," Mrs Crawford said at last, moving away and drawing the curtains. "There's no rush."

She waited until Mrs Crawford had gone downstairs and only then, still in her nightgown, staring from the steamed-up window at the bare branches of the trees, looking at the heavy grey of the sky, seeing the sparkle of the frosty streets, thinking of Maggie being laid to rest soon in the cold ground of the cemetery up in Preston, only then did she allow herself to weep.

***

That was not the end of the bad news that year. Six months later, her father was killed in an accident at the mill, Mrs Crawford sparing her the details, and her mother died supposedly of a broken heart within weeks. Mrs Flintoff was of the opinion that you could not die of a broken heart but recalling her mum's words, how she could not live without him, Vanessa was not so sure. In the space of a few months, her mother had lost her husband and her dearest Maggie and, to all intents, Nessa too.

According to Mrs Flintoff, Lizzie had left the old house, apparently well enough these days to look after herself. But, with Maggie gone, Vanessa felt very responsible for her. Sitting at the mahogany desk in Mrs Crawford's sitting room, looking out onto the street where the trees were now in full leaf, she pulled a sheet of notepaper towards her and started to write a letter to her sister via the usual channel, although she suspected that Lizzie would never want it to be read to her.

"Is your letter finished?" Mrs Crawford asked, coming into the room later. "I have several waiting to be posted so I can include yours."

Vanessa clutched the letter to her chest. "Can I ask Lizzie to come to stay awhile with us? I'm not sure she can look after herself. She could help out and she could sleep up in the attic. You wouldn't have to pay her much."

"The money is of no concern," Mrs Crawford said with a slight smile. "The difficulty is your new identity, my dear. And, may I say that Lizzie is simply too stupid to be let in on the secret. We would both be discredited and we will never find a suitable husband for you. I am afraid we cannot take the risk."

Lizzie too stupid? Vanessa bit back a retort to that high handed comment. She was right of course for it would be a grave mistake for Lizzie to come here but she would send a letter of sorts anyway and a little money.

Now that Mrs Crawford was confident Vanessa could make her way in the upper eons of society, now that Mrs Crawford's plans for her were in their ascendency, now that several things were underway, they simply could not risk Lizzie making a complete and utter mess of it.

Even though it hit her conscience hard, Vanessa knew there was no alternative.

Lizzie would have to fend for herself.

CHAPTER FIVE

It was at the Old Vic theatre that she was, at last, introduced to the man she would marry.

"Ah Florence, there you are..." a large lady with a jutting chin powered their way, accompanied by a fair-haired gentleman with a pleasant demeanour. "How wonderful! And this must be your charge, dearest Vanessa." She beamed at her, her well supported bosom heaving, an emerald necklace dangling around her neck. "My dear, I've heard so much about you."

The meeting with Theodore was arranged by Mrs Crawford and his mother, Henrietta Asher. It was an embarrassment to both she and Theodore when the older ladies departed, leaving them alone.

"So, you are related to Mrs Crawford, Miss Jones?"

"Yes, although vaguely," she said. "Mrs Crawford kindly took me in after my dear parents..." she paused. "... after they died." For a moment, she was reminded that they had died, her real parents as well as her pretend ones and her eyes filled with unexpected tears and she saw the sudden sympathy in his eyes, liked him for it. Kindness was a wonderful attribute and almost made up for the fact that, in appearance, he was hardly her ideal.

"I am so sorry, Miss Jones…"

"Vanessa, please."

"Vanessa and you must call me Theodore. It's jolly hard luck to lose your parents. My father died years ago but I'm lucky to have my mother."

"Yes. She seems charming."

"She's a great supporter of the Arts. Between you and me…" he lowered his voice. "I wouldn't expect too much of this play. It goes on and on and it's dreadfully dull."

They exchanged a smile before looking across the room to where the two ladies in question were standing chatting, firing occasional conspiratorial glances in their direction.

"What do you think of the Duke of Windsor marrying that Wallace woman? My mother is appalled and quite horrified that he should land his brother in it."

"He must love her very much," she said. "To give up the throne."

"Yes he must. Good luck to the fellow I say although I have to say duty is duty and I would never have done such a thing and nor would most honourable men." He clicked open a silver cigarette case and offered her a cigarette which she refused but, as he lit up his own, it gave her the opportunity to observe him more closely. Theodore – Teddy - Asher was about the same height as herself but broad with powerful shoulders, a man you could faint into with great ease for he might gather you up in his arms as if you were the lightest of feathers. He would become portly with age like his mother but, as yet, there was little sign of that. He was no Clark Gable but he had a certain quiet charm.

For the visit to the theatre this evening, she was wearing a divine primrose satin evening dress, a cascade of frills fluttering down the side of the skirt and, with her hair pinned up, a simple row of pearls round her neck she felt wonderful. She was delighted also with her gorgeous silk evening bag with its exquisite embroidered decoration, carrying it proudly for it was something to be noticed but not drawing unnecessary attention to it as per Mrs Crawford's instructions. Drawing attention to an expensive item would be vulgar.

The bell sounded for the start of the play and, although she felt like tearing ahead to her seat, she made her way infinitely slowly, giving Theodore a little nod of supreme indifference, barely acknowledging him when she saw him later in the evening accompanied by his mother. Do not appear too interested, Mrs Crawford had said, for that puts the gentlemen off. On the other hand, a cool glance their way greatly excites them.

Vanessa thought of it as flirting and quite why she was doing it, to a man like Theodore, she had no idea but she wanted to please Mrs Crawford and, as they drove home, she was delighted that she had.

***

"Do you like him?" Mrs Crawford asked, eyes twinkling, once they were indoors, relaxing and having a hot drink.

"I do. He seems charming."

"Wasn't he splendidly attired? He's rather a dandy." Mrs Crawford looked quite girlish for a moment. "His mother wishes Teddy to marry. It's to do with an inheritance from an aunt who adored him but it is dependent on him being married. If he doesn't marry, he risks losing it so it's become somewhat imperative he finds a wife. Henrietta despairs because it doesn't seem to worry him in the slightest. He is an architect and makes quite enough money from his own efforts but she feels it would be tragic for him to throw away such a substantial sum and I believe he has finally come round to her way of thinking. It would be quite convenient for him to have a wife, improve his social standing, and knock any rumours on the head."

"Rumours?"

"Yes, rumours. The problem is, despite all Henrietta's efforts, he has shown little interest in the opposite sex..." she coughed and a blush flooded her neck and face. "I don't know, my dear, if you know about such things but some gentlemen are not very interested in ladies."

"Aren't they?" she gasped. "Why not?"

"Oh, my dear..." Mrs Crawford did not look directly at her. "It's not important. He will be kind and gentle with you and you will live in splendour for he has a lovely house. Theodore is agreeable, I believe, to marrying you."

"But he only met me tonight," she blurted out. "How can he want to marry me? He doesn't know me."

"I know you, my dear, and I have assured Mrs Asher that you will make an admirable wife for him."

She watched as Mrs Crawford picked up her cup and sipped her milk, unaware it seemed of the enormity of what she was saying.

"I don't love him," Vanessa said for it had to be said. "I quite like him but I don't love him and I want to marry for love."

"Like your mother?" Mrs Crawford said tartly.

"Well, yes…" she bit her lip. "I don't know Theodore at all," she went on. "I don't want to marry him, Auntie Florence."

"Mrs Crawford, please…" she murmured, looking pained. "I do hope you are not going to be difficult. Why should you imagine you have any choice in the matter? I owe Mrs Asher a favour …"

"Whatever for?"

"It is none of your business, Vanessa." She held up her hand to indicate there would be no further discussion on that subject. "So, when she suggested it, I was delighted to agree to you meeting him. They are a worthy family and she is quite exhausted with her efforts, desperate to have a grandchild, so she is happy to take my word that you will be a good match for him."

"Why am I a good match?"

"You are young and beautiful, bright but not overly intelligent and you know how to behave. There will be no trouble from you and I have given Mrs Asher that assurance." She leaned forward and in the now dim light her eyes were cold and Vanessa recoiled, seeing her afresh, seeing her as Maggie had seen her, the not overly intelligent really grating. "I could throw you out tomorrow, my dear," she said, her voice like ice, low and infinitely menacing.

"You wouldn't do that?"

"I would not choose to do it but I owe you nothing more," Mrs Crawford said and, despite the warmth of the fire Vanessa felt a shiver deep inside. "But you owe me a good deal. So you would be a very wise young lady if you do as I ask. If everything goes to plan Theodore will propose marriage shortly and you will accept."

"But…"

Mrs Crawford put a finger to her lips and shook her head.

She saw she was trapped. She liked Mrs Crawford well enough for she had indeed been very kind to her but this evening she had seen a different side and she was reminded of Maggie and how she had always been right about people.

She was but a plaything to Mrs Crawford, a beautiful doll she could dress and look after but when it came to it, she could be tossed aside and left to gather dust.

***

She was at an evening recital with Mrs Crawford. A string quartet was playing and Vanessa was trying her best to pay attention but her mind was wandering. Things were progressing with Theodore although he was absent this evening. The more she saw of him, the more she liked him. He kissed her hand so charmingly, raising it to his lips and smiling and he called her my lovely which delighted her.

The proposal was due any day and she was going to accept, not because Mrs Crawford had been rather brusque about it but because she now wanted to.

The audience broke into applause as the concert drew to a close and they moved around the room, Mrs Crawford disappearing with a friend so that, momentarily, Vanessa was alone.

"Nessa... Nessa Cookson if I live and die."

She spun round and came face to face with Tony Walsh.

***

The admiration in his eyes competed with the shock.

"I never thought I would see you again," he said. "Nobody knew where you went and I never told a soul about seeing you that morning. You

84

look beautiful, Nessa. You are easily the most beautiful woman in the room."

He had always been good at the sweet talk but her heart soared at the words nonetheless, managing a shaky smile.

"I am Vanessa now," she told him. "Vanessa Jones from the Welsh borders. Mrs Crawford is a distant relative who kindly took me under her wing when my parents died. My father…" she hesitated then carried briskly on. "He was a country solicitor and my poor mother was an invalid. They are both dead."

He nodded. He looked much the same but he still had that lopsided grin which he now employed to great effect.

"Well, well… and how beautifully you speak."

"And you," she acknowledged. "You've lost your accent too."

"Have I?" he seemed surprised as he glanced round and drew her into a corner where they might enjoy some degree of privacy. "I work here now."

"Are you still a reporter?"

"Sort of," he said.

"Which paper?"

"Illustrated London News."

"I see."

"I visit my mother from time to time although she's never forgiven me for moving away. As for you, you broke your mother's heart. You left her a note but you never went back. She took to her bed for days afterwards. My mother helped out and your sister Maggie too. Your mother was never the same again."

"I know. It broke my heart too," she confessed. "It was very hard but I couldn't go back for the funerals but I thought about them all."

"You will be pleased to hear that your sister Lizzie is managing on her own."

She caught the sharpness in his tone, knew that he thought she had been neglectful of her sister which of course she had.

"I've written to her and sent her some money," she told him. "But I don't know if the letters get through and she would need helping reading them. But I live this life now and I am soon to be engaged to be married," she added.

"Who is the lucky man?" The light in his eyes dulled.

"Theodore, Teddy Asher. I don't suppose you know him?"

"I know of him," he said with a slight smile. "I know the Club he frequents and some of the members."

"Are you a member?"

"God, no." His smile broadened but did not reach his eyes. "I was never good enough for you, was I?"

"It wasn't that. I wish I could have loved you, Tony."

He nodded. "So do I. Do you love him?"

"He's very kind," she murmured. "I shall do my best to be a good wife."

"Dear God. Can you hear yourself?" He touched her arm but she drew back sharply knowing what it must look like if anybody was watching for their conversation was intense enough as it was without touching becoming involved. "By the way, I was sorry about what happened to your father," he went on. "It made the front page of the local rag."

"What did happen? Nobody would tell me the details."

"You don't want to know."

"I do. Please tell me."

"He was hit by a flying shuttle and very nearly decapitated," he said. "That means…"

"I know what it means," she hissed, irritated because like most men in that Lancashire world he didn't think women had a brain in their heads.

"There was an inquest but it was ruled to be an accident but I believe the whole thing was hushed up. The machine was faulty and that bloody man, George Whitlock, knew."

A vision rose up, a very unpleasant one of her father lying on the mill floor and she took a deep breath, swaying as Tony steadied her with his arm.

"Sorry but you wanted to know," he said and, across the room, she saw Mrs Crawford and another lady heading towards them.

"Don't give me away," she urged. "Please don't do that."

"Don't you know me at all?" He took her hand briefly, looked into her eyes and she saw the pain in them. "Goodbye Nessa," he said and strode off before the ladies arrived.

"Who was that gentleman?" Mrs Crawford asked with a frown. "You were deep in conversation."

She shrugged, smiled, indicating that he was nobody in particular.

She wondered if Mrs Crawford had recognised him but, if she had, she made no mention of it then or later.

CHAPTER SIX

They were to spend their honeymoon in Paris, her trousseau happily provided by Mrs Crawford. There were sets of pyjamas, under-slips, camiknickers and camisoles, all matching in ivory satin with pink lace trim and a pale green coloured crepe de Chine wrap for her to wear at breakfast. There was also a selection of afternoon dresses and a couple of evening gowns.

Vanessa was incredibly nervous. Theodore loved her in his way, she knew that, and he had always been so considerate, kissing her gently and looking at her tenderly today as he placed his ring on her finger. If he was impatient to take their sexual relationship further, he did not show it, content with chaste kisses it would seem.

The wedding had been a discreet affair but that suited both Mrs Crawford and Vanessa. A short betrothal announcement followed later by the wedding announcement in the society pages was all that was needed for people to know that Theodore Asher, a bachelor of means, was no longer available.

The evening before her wedding, Mrs Crawford had talked alarmingly and with a flushed face about sex.

"I am so sorry but you must do as he says," she said, taking hold of Vanessa's hand. "I hope it won't come as too much of a shock, my dear, but it will get easier I assure you and it is a price we ladies have to pay. We must hope you are with child soon so that will spare you all that sort of thing for a few months."

It was those words as much as anything that explained why Mrs Crawford's marriage had failed if that was how she viewed physical love. In the end, Vanessa ended up reassuring Mrs Crawford that all would be well. Teddy was a gentle man, she told her, and although his kisses did not set her on fire as kisses seemed to do for the ladies on the cinema screen, she was perfectly happy and indeed looking forward to being a married lady.

"Welcome to the Asher family, Vanessa dear," Henrietta exclaimed after the ceremony. "I am so looking forward to becoming a grandmother," she added in a low voice. "I know I should not say such things but I do hope you have a child quickly. It will do wonders for my darling Teddy to be a father."

Vanessa, who hadn't actually thought of having a baby for some time yet had no option but to nod her agreement for it would seem that both Mrs Crawford and her new mother-in-law expected it of her.

From now on, she would be known as Teddy's wife, Mrs Theodore Asher and that was very much that.

***

Today, her wedding day, she had flown in an aeroplane for the first time on Imperial Airways, and although it had been cold and noisy and she had a brief terrible earache just before they landed, it had also been so exciting to be up there above the clouds.

Theodore had introduced her on the aeroplane as my wife and those words set a little thrill running through her, the air stewardess's look suitably respectful as she attended to madam. Theodore knew how to behave, and she followed his lead although she did smile sympathetically at the poor girl when she became a little flustered and brought the wrong drink.

"My wife asked for a Pink Pearl cocktail," Theodore said at once as the drink was presented to her, his voice terse.

"No, no, this is just fine thank you," she said, touching his arm and smiling his grumpiness away.

She had high hopes after the romantic dinner that evening under the Parisian night sky but the inevitable lovemaking that followed was a short and sweaty experience with Theodore telling her when it was over that she had done very well and he hoped that it had not been too much of an ordeal for her.

Afterwards, she filled a bath with scented cubes and had a long bubbly soak, wiping away tears of frustration with a damp hand. And soon, from the bedroom, she heard the sound of contented snoring.

Thereafter the pattern was set. She knew then that the comfortable life Theodore provided was not quite enough. She wished for true love, real passion and William Whitlock stuck in her head like a stubborn paste, impossible to dislodge however much she tried to shake it free.

***

As the new Mrs Theodore Asher, she moved into his house in London, a house complete with a small staff. Being waited on hand and foot did not come easily to her and, at the beginning she made one or two little gaffes in her dealings with the servants. She saw how he dealt with them deploring the sometimes short shrift he gave them, so she compromised in the way she treated them for a kind smile went a long way and she wanted a happy home. The Asher's were further up the society ladder than Mrs Crawford and a girl was appointed to be her maid, greeting her each day with a little respectful bob. It was a surprise how quickly Vanessa found herself getting used to this as, with the passing of each day, her past life was erased from her memory even further. The little episode with Tony Walsh had been a reminder, however, and she hoped she had seen the last of him for, if he had a mind to, he could cause her a lot of trouble. She reassured herself knowing that he still loved her and would never willingly hurt her.

A surprise awaited her as she learned that, in addition to this house, there was a house in the Lancashire hills for it transpired that Henrietta Asher was originally a Bleasdale from Lancashire. The house had been owned by her family for years and years and one day it would pass to Theodore.

When they visited the north, and they soon did for he was anxious to show Snape Hall to her, she was unable to avoid spending a day in Preston. With her hair swept up, her fashionable clothes and jewellery, she knew nobody would recognise her. She was tempted to test the success of her new persona by buying an umbrella from the shop but lost her nerve at the last for surely she would never pass that test.

It was not a comfortable experience, so when Theodore suggested a further visit, she pleaded a dreadful migraine. It meant a good deal of fussing and lying down in a darkened room with Teddy most concerned about her and she felt badly about that, deceiving him, but then her lies were so numerous that another one, a little one, hardly mattered.

A year after they married, she and Theodore went to Egypt on holiday, a decision that was to mean yet another momentous shift in her life for, it was there that, once more, she met her darling man, William Whitlock.

***

The holiday needed a lot of organizing, passports and visits to the Egyptian legation and so on and there were a few difficulties because she did not have all the necessary papers – of course she did not - but Theodore had contacts, fresh papers were produced and it was waived through.

"Isn't this so exciting, darling?" he said, coming into the bedroom as she was sorting through her jewellery.

"Are you sure it will be safe to take any of this, Teddy?"

"Perfectly. There are secure lockers on board and everything is insured."

That was not the point. Handling her jewellery, picking up a fine silver bangle, she was reminded of Lizzie and it was enough to make her sit down and silently finger it. This one was genuine silver and she wondered if Lizzie was still wearing hers.

"You're not still worried about the sea journey, are you?" Theodore asked, sensing her mood.

Of course she was worried about the journey, she told him. There was a long sea journey to undergo and she could not swim and what would they do if the ship sank? Ships did sink.

"We are not crossing the ocean, my lovely," Theodore said, looking at her with fond exasperation. "Just the Mediterranean."

"That makes no difference," she said, knowing she was getting herself into a state of silly alarm. "Maggie always said…" she stopped.

"Take no notice of what Maggie said," he said, assuming her to be a maid. "The crossing will be smooth as silk. And if it isn't, if it upsets my wife, I shall insist on a refund."

Fortunately, the trip was uneventful, from the time they set foot on the boat train to Marseilles until they arrived, yesterday, to embark on the steamer. She had hopes that perhaps in a new environment, away from London and business, Theodore might unwind a little for with him it was forever business although he did spend a lot of time in the evenings and sometimes overnight at his Club.

She did not mind when he did that. Having the big bed to herself was a joy for Teddy was apt to throw his arms around during the night and as for the snoring...

Being alone was utter bliss.

***

One of the first things Theodore did was to check the passenger register, not the least surprised that there was a good sprinkling of the aristocracy, some of whom were looking thoroughly bored already, most of them complaining about the heat and dust.

"Oh dear." Vanessa smiled. "I hope they won't spoil things for us."

Mrs Crawford had prepared her for dealing with such ladies by explaining that very often they were not very bright and that it would never occur to them that Vanessa was anything other than whom she was meant to be.

She picked up a fan and wafted it about, calming herself. "It is hot," she admitted. "But it has been so cold and wet at home that I love it."

"Good. I don't want you complaining too. Once we set sail all will be well as there will be a cooling breeze. Please don't worry for you will charm the gentlemen, my dear, and the ladies will be quite envious of your beauty and your lovely dresses."

Through the mirror, she smiled at him for he had bought her several new dresses, one in emerald green satin which had of course reminded her instantly of Lizzie and the borrowed frock There was just something about this colour that seemed to make her skin luminous, give her eyes a sparkle and, as any woman would, she delighted in that.

Henrietta had helped her choose it. Her mother-in-law was increasingly indiscreet these days, always with half an eye on Vanessa's waistline looking for signs of pregnancy. Shopping with Henrietta was not easy as that lady, stubborn chin at the fore, swept into shops with Vanessa just one step behind. She caught the anxiety of the shop-girls anxious to please this formidable lady. Theodore would have nothing to do with such trivia, more than happy for his mother to accompany her.

She loved this emerald green dress as soon as she tried it on in the dressing room in the shop although the memory of her mother fussing around her with that other green dress did dull her excitement a little. She had to take a breath, remembering the age it had taken her mother to fasten all the fiddly buttons with her arthritic fingers and the way it had been so tight. Looking back, it was probably the most uncomfortable dress she had ever worn but her mother had been so proud of her that day and it had shown in her eyes. She had never said I love you but she had loved her in her way. Why hadn't she said those words, not only to her mother but to Maggie for, if love was to be measured, Maggie had the lion's share.

In the privacy of the dressing room, the painful jolt into the past was enough to blur her vision momentarily.

"Do you need any help, madam?"

"No thank you. I am just adjusting it." She took a final look at herself before stepping out hoping for Henrietta's approval this time.

"What do you think of this one, mama?" she asked, still struggling with the mama but Henrietta had insisted.

The gasps of delight from the salesgirl – to be expected – and, more importantly, Henrietta were proof enough that it was a success and, with spirits thus raised, two more dresses were quickly added.

"This will be a second honeymoon for you," Henrietta told Vanessa, as they exited the shop with their purchases. "Teddy worries too much about work and you must help him relax. The sun will work wonders for that and who knows…" her eyes twinkled. "It's nigh on time, my dear Vanessa, that you have a child. The Asher name is relying on you and it will be doubly joyful if you have a boy."

You need two to tango, Vanessa might have told her although of course she did not but after a year, their lovemaking was practically non-existent. However, like her mother-in-law, she was relying on this cruise to relax him sufficiently and if an exotic holiday failed to do that then what on earth would?

She loved Theodore for his kindness but sometimes she wanted him to be more dynamic, to sweep her up in his arms, to show some passion and she hid a sigh now as she watched him getting ready for the first evening under Egyptian skies.

"We also have a cotton magnate on board," Theodore went on, fussing with the selection of tie. "He's from Lancashire. From Preston. A Mr William Whitlock and wife, Ruby House, Preston. Flamboyant signature."

Vanessa was sitting at the dressing table brushing her hair and very nearly dropped the brush. William Whitlock! On board this very vessel?

"I expect he'll be a bit brash, these northern fellows often are, particularly mill owners," Theodore said with a sniff "But we should make a point of speaking with them for others might not. After all, they live not far from our house in the north and it is an excellent opportunity to get to know them. You should cultivate new friends, Vanessa," he added. "Mama says we must entertain more. If we find them agreeable then we will certainly have them over to Snape Hall for the weekend."

Vanessa put down her hairbrush. That must never happen and she would make certain it did not but, in the meantime, she would have to use all her acting skills perfected over these last few years and be pleasant and courteous towards them.

As they went into the cocktail lounge, she noticed him at once, catching a glance and looking away, her mouth suddenly dry, but even turned away from him she could sense something, the impulses coming from him to her like hot daggers and, when she dared another glance, to her horror he interpreted it immediately with a half smile and a slight bow. He was almost the same several years on, the same smile certainly, the same upright posture, the hair every bit as dark and lush as before.

She had come a long way from sitting in the corridor in Ruby House waiting for Mrs Bamber to call her in. Now, she was William's equal and she was confident that he would not recognise her from a fleeting glance many years ago. She recognised him but that was quite different.

His new wife, for it quickly transpired that he was on honeymoon, was tall and slender and red haired with the pale freckled face to match, although her peach gown was stylish and she dimpled rather attractively when she smiled. On closer inspection, she had eyes of an unusual grey green with sandy lashes and most surprisingly of all she was very young; a mere eighteen.

"May I introduce my wife Vanessa…" Theodore said proudly, his hand on her waist as they eventually stood before William and Kathleen. "We live in London but we have a home near Chipping; Snape Hall. Do you know it?"

"Indeed. I know the area well," William Whitlock said, his eyes fixed on Vanessa. She knew it was unwise to meet his gaze directly so, following the brief handshake, she turned her attention to his wife.

"How lovely! We're practically neighbours," Kathleen said, eyes shining. "Do you love the countryside?"

"My wife is not familiar with the area at all." Theodore answered the question for her as Vanessa struggled to think of something appropriate to say. Uncomfortably she could feel his eyes on her and already it felt inappropriate in a newly married gentleman. She drew her attention back to Theodore, taking the opportunity to gaze at him in a wifely fashion as he continued. "She's from the Welsh borders originally. Aren't you, dearest?"

She nodded as Kathleen smiled.

It was the cocktail hour and they proceeded to choose theirs. Having become familiar with a range of cocktails, Vanessa opted for an Aviation with both gentlemen ordering a Gin Rickey.

"I don't drink," Kathleen said, requesting lemonade. "My mama considers it vulgar for a lady to drink."

She caught William's bemused glance towards his wife and Kathleen, realising perhaps what she had just said, flushed that uncomfortable shade of the red-head.

"I'm sorry. I didn't mean that you..." she laughed uncertainly, looking at Vanessa who immediately gave her a big smile as their drinks arrived for, despite the odd circumstances, she could not help but like this girl.

William, making amends, ushered his wife away, his hand at her slender waist.

"Nice fellow. Silly wife," Theodore murmured to their retreating backs. "For a girl who has been to finishing school in Switzerland, she seems surprisingly unsophisticated, don't you think?"

"She seems charming, Teddy," Vanessa said, determined to give the girl a chance. Finishing school? How did Teddy know that already but then he had been chatting to other people and there were few secrets on board.

Other than her own of course.

It was a relief to disperse and mingle with the other guests as the music started up, the pianist playing a selection of well known songs beginning with Smoke Gets in Your Eyes. She had learned that Kathleen did not smoke either but then Vanessa did only rarely. It was a useful social skill, Mrs Crawford had said, because you did not want to stand out if other guests were enjoying a smoke.

Vanessa spent the rest of the evening trying to avoid William and his bride. Looking at her, at the easy way she looked at her husband and laughed, confidence regained, Vanessa felt a pinch of jealousy so intense it made her chest ache. She did her best to conceal it and later as they all went their separate ways she was back in control of her emotions and able to give Kathleen a little cheery wave and a very big smile.

***

Somehow she got through that first meeting reassured that, if she concentrated, remembered who she was or rather who she was supposed to be then she could rise above her feelings for this man. It was astonishing that, after all these years, they remained as strong as ever.

However, his wife, the very young Mrs Whitlock, befriended her and it would be churlish and indeed impossible within the confines of this pleasure steamer to snub her. And so, early one morning after they had breakfasted, Vanessa saw Kathleen heading purposefully towards her on deck where Vanessa was sitting under a parasol enjoying the outdoors before the heat of the day made it impossible.

There were daily excursions to look forward to and yesterday they had staggered about in the sand going from one tomb to another. They were protected by Egyptian policemen on white Arab ponies who seemed to spend all their time flicking whips at the many beggars. Vanessa had felt so sorry for them but Theodore had warned her not to give them a penny. A fellow traveller Lady Palmer had turned her face away and refused to look at them.

"I'm so looking forward to staying at the hotel tonight," Kathleen said, taking a seat on a deck-chair beside Vanessa. "This boat is making me feel nauseous. Oh my gracious, is that lemonade?"

"Yes. Would you like a glass?"

"Yes please, Mrs Asher."

"Do call me Vanessa."

"And you must call me Kathleen. Do you call your husband Theodore or do you have a nickname for him?" she asked eyes merry.

Rather taken aback, Vanessa acknowledged that yes she did sometimes call him Teddy in private.

"Teddy?" Kathleen clapped her hands and giggled. "Oh thanks awfully." She took the glass Vanessa passed her and gulped the liquid in a not very ladylike fashion, some of it spilling down her chin so that she hastily dabbed at it with a napkin. "Sorry… I'm so thirsty. Isn't this heat appalling?

The boat is lovely but so cramped. Putting on a gown is so difficult, isn't it? I believe the hotel is very swanky and we shall have a suite. I can't wait to get there."

"Yes it will be lovely to be on dry land again."

Kathleen pulled up the skirt of her dress, black silk with a bright floral pattern, showing off her shoes by moving her slender foot from side to side.

"Do you like them?" she asked. "They are buckskin and very uncomfortable but I adore them."

"They are very nice," Vanessa told her with a smile at the way of young girls and, how at that tender age, she would have died for a pair of white buckskin shoes.

It did not take long to work out that, even though she did not realize it herself, Kathleen, too, had been coerced into marriage, it having been decided that it was time William was married, George Whitlock like Henrietta being desperate for a grandson. Kathleen who was from a wealthy old-money background talked happily about how she had fallen in love at first sight with William and she described in detail her wedding at St Saviour's Church.

"Do you live at Ruby House now?" Vanessa interrupted her in full flow, realising her mistake at once as she caught Kathleen's puzzled look.

"Oh. You know of it?"

"Oh no, no. I think the gentlemen may have talked of it," she said airily.

"We don't live there yet but we shall move in after the honeymoon." Kathleen's face brightened. "My father-in-law Mr Whitlock and Martha, William's sister, are moving to a smaller house and I shall be mistress of Ruby House. It is so huge and I shall have so much to do. I have never dealt with staff before but my mother and Miss Whitlock have given me advice and instruction. We married ladies lead such busy lives, don't we?"

She was not so much older than Kathleen but at that moment sipping her lemonade in the Egyptian heat Vanessa felt hundreds of years older.

CHAPTER SEVEN

The next day, in the grounds of the hotel at Luxor, she found herself quite by chance alone with William. They greeted each other and then, to her chagrin, he started to walk beside her and she had no option but to continue her stroll.

"This is a charming hotel, don't you think?" he said, looking back towards it. "Kathleen is very taken with it. She is thrilled to be off the boat and has already deposited all her dresses with the housekeeper to be cleaned. She is rather appalled that it costs 3/6 to have a dress cleaned. She is thrifty," he added with a smile. "She gets it from her mama."

"Where is your wife?"

"She has gone on the trip," he said. "I was going to go with her but she was happy to go off in the company of Lady Palmer and I couldn't face another donkey trek."

"Nor could I," she told him. "It's far too dusty and I feel sorry for the donkeys. Lady Palmer is…" she paused, struggling to be polite for Lady Palmer was an enormous lady and the poor donkey who was allocated to her had looked quite miserable when she was hauled upon him. "… an impressive presence," she finished lamely.

He laughed. "She is certainly that."

"I hope your wife has some ointment with her for the bugs," she went on. "I was bitten the other day."

"I am sorry. We have been lucky so far. You need a flywhisk."

"Yes. I must get one."

"Kathleen has to try to keep out of the sun. Her colouring, you know. As for the bugs, they have taken a first-aid box with them so all will be well."

Just talking of being bitten made her sore shoulder throb. Theodore had gently soothed it last night, rubbing cream into the affected area, and in the bedroom of the hotel, sitting beside him wearing a silk wrap she had felt aroused by the gentle pressure of his hands on her skin and made it plain to him. However, he had merely adjusted her wrap, kissed the top of her head and gone into the bathroom and afterwards, turned away from her in the big bed. Frustratingly aroused, her body tingling still from his touch, she had made one final effort, curling up against his back, her lace-trimmed coffee coloured nightdress a silken barrier between her body and his for, in this heat, he slept only in pyjama trousers but even as her own breathing became ragged, she felt him shifting about uncomfortably, moving away a little, and then he said goodnight, sleep well dearest, and that was clear as clear.

The humiliation was complete.

"Where is your husband?"

"I have no idea why but he's gone to look at some camels," she told him. "They are nice creatures, rather dignified with lovely eyes and the longest eyelashes, don't you think, but they smell a little too powerfully for my liking and they can be quite grumpy."

"I agree. Do you smoke?"

"Occasionally."

He opened his cigarette case and offered her one, lighting it for her and they stood under the shade of a tree and smoked in silence for a while. The distance between them was politely observed but she could feel a palpable tension and a slight break in his voice as he chatted on. It seemed he was finding the cruise a trial full as it was of rich, dull people, their wealth inherited, their snobbery locked in. It had made the atmosphere on board a little sour and he was grateful that she and Mr Asher had taken the trouble to befriend them.

"Oh dear." She could find nothing to say to that for it had never occurred to her that the Whitlocks who were looked on as royalty in Preston could be considered in any way vulgar. And yet, hadn't Theodore said as much. Her husband was such a thoughtful man. Thoughtful and utterly without passion.

"My wife says she does not care a ha'penny but I mind a lot." he said and she could see the angry glint in his eyes. "My great grandfather was a patron of the arts and a great benefactor and we continue that tradition, Vanessa. I know you don't know Preston but it's not a bad town. We own a few terraces and the workers live there in perfectly adequate accommodation. "

She nodded, wanting to change this subject… now… but not sure how to do it.

"There are sadly a few accidents in the mill. I intend to bring in a lot of new safety measures when I take over. A lot of the equipment needs replacing but my father is always thinking about the pennies."

She remembered the accident, the horrible accident that had killed her father but said nothing.

"Forgive me. I'm sorry to burden you with my troubles," he went on. "I feel melancholy and when you feel like this, it is as if the whole world is against you. I don't like to talk of such things to Kathleen because she finds it so upsetting. And, after all, it is our honeymoon so I ought to be full of joy. And I am, of course," he added hastily.

"We all feel melancholy sometimes," she said. "If you'll excuse me, I am going to my room to take a rest. I need to cool down a little."

"Stay a while," he said, breaking into a smile. "I know I am not good company this afternoon but we can take tea on the veranda if you wish. It is cooler there in the shade and with a bit of luck it might cheer me up so that I am not such dreadful company."

She hesitated but there was no harm in that, in full view of everybody and a cup of hot sweet tea did appeal. "Thank you. I would like that."

***

"Why did you marry him?" William asked.

It was such an impertinent question that she gasped, drawing a handkerchief from her bag and pressing it against her mouth. The tables were emptying and soon they were alone hidden away in a corner of the veranda. It was a scented heaven of white and lilac flowers rambling up a wooden support. It was still hot but bearable now and she had no need of her fan. For a few seconds, Vanessa closed her eyes and breathed deeply and when she opened them, William was watching her, smiling reassuringly. When she did not answer, he began to speak.

"I married Kathleen because it was time to get married and I grew tired of my sister's constant pestering. I am still treated like the baby of the family. I could have gone against their wishes, Martha and my father, but he would probably have disowned me and I have a strong family loyalty. I am his son and I want to succeed in the business."

"Yes. Family is so important," she said. What was he saying? That he had only married Kathleen because of family loyalty?

"I'm sorry. Forgive me for discussing my family business. I trust you will be discreet?"

"Oh yes. Of course," she promised with a smile.

"And, Kathleen as you see is an enchanting girl. She will be a great asset. Martha approves of Kathleen and her family."

How awful! To be approved of rather than liked. She found herself irritated on Kathleen's behalf. Imagine being saddled with a sister-in-law like Martha Whitlock and, unless she was hiding it well, Kathleen did not look as if she had the gumption to stand up to a woman like that. She would be trodden into the ground in her role of mistress of Ruby House unless she stood up for herself.

"Your wife is charming and very pretty." Vanessa drew herself upright, as the waiter arrived with their tea.

"I'm pleased that you and Kathleen get on so well. When you come up to your house in Lancashire you must visit us."

"Thank you," she murmured, knowing that must never be. "You must visit us, too, you and your wife," she said, confident that such an invitation would never be issued.

He inclined his head. "Now I have told you why I married Kathleen so tell me why you married Theodore?"

She took a careful sip of the hot tea feeling his eyes on her.

"He is a kind man," she said. "And he loves me."

"Ah. And do you love him?"

Tony Walsh had asked the very same question but she would not answer it this time in quite the same way.

"I certainly do love my husband although, Mr Whitlock, if I may say so it is none of your business," she said in a voice that would cut through ice, rattling her cup down in its saucer before rising to her feet, half amused by the sudden mortified expression on his face. She scooped up her hat as he scraped back his chair and stood up.

"I didn't mean to offend you," he said, his face a picture of remorse. "Please stay and finish your tea."

"I think not. Good day."

She edged her way out, walking quickly into the cool foyer of the hotel, her footsteps loud on the tiled floor.

All in all, she thought she had handled that rather well.

***

It was the last day on board the steamer and the heat of the day lingered, although there was the slightest of breezes wafting from shore.

Alone on deck with the boat moored for the night, Vanessa waited for the sunset. She never noticed sunsets at home but here against the broad sweep of the African sky they were spectacular and within a few moments she was rewarded as the enormous ball of the sun squashed against the horizon like a flattened orange. Beyond the riverbank stretched miles of Sahara dunes, fine wispy sand which got everywhere, in the very creases of your skin, underneath your fingernails, so that even after a bath you still felt gritty.

She could hear voices from the lounge where people were assembling already for cocktails before dinner. She had told Theodore she needed some air and although he had offered to accompany her, he seemed relieved when she said she was happy to be alone for a while. He was establishing a few contacts, he told her, useful people in his world and he seemed very pleased that they were reacting so well to her. She was not to concern herself with the business; her job was simply to look beautiful when she was with them.

It suited her well. Avoid big opinions, Mrs Crawford had told her, for then people remember you and we don't want too much scrutiny.

Leaning on the deck rail overlooking the river and the darkening view, it was some time before she sensed that somebody was standing close by and, turning, her dress rustling, she saw that it was William.

"Just look at that sunset," he said. "If I were an artist, I would like to paint it."

"So would I."

"I haven't had the chance to speak to you since that afternoon at the hotel," he said, rushing the words. "Please accept my apologies for upsetting you. I never meant to. As I said, I was in a melancholy mood."

"Apology accepted."

"Good. I wouldn't like us to part on bad terms not if we are to see each other again occasionally when we get home."

"We do live in London," she reminded him. "And I'm not sure when we will be visiting the house up there," she said, hoping he took the hint. "Theodore is very busy with a new project."

"This time next week this will all be a distant dream," he said, coming closer and leaning against the deck-rail at her side.

"Is Kathleen feeling any better?"

"A little. She will probably be up for dinner. I am sorry I dragged her here because the heat's been too much for her and there's much to do at home. When we get back, she will have to take over the running of the house because I will be fully occupied at the mill. My father should really be thinking about retiring but he clings on and he isn't in the best of health."

"I'm sorry to hear that. You must not worry about Kathleen. She will manage very well and she tells me that your sister Martha will be there to help," she added mischievously.

"Indeed. I gather you ladies have been talking. I am so glad that Martha will be looking after father when they move. She will miss Ruby House but she is hoping that a move to the country will settle father a little and stop him worrying about the mill. Is Theodore looking forward to returning home?" he asked with an abrupt change of subject.

"Yes. He has much to do."

She looked down at their hands on the smooth polished rail, then below to the gently lapping water of the Nile and shivered, pulling her silver-fringed evening wrap tighter round her shoulders. Lights twinkled on the shore and her diamond engagement ring glittered.

"You look lovely this evening. You know, when we were introduced, I had the oddest feeling we have met before. Have we met before, Vanessa?"

"No, I don't believe so."

"I've seen you before somewhere," he said. "I would never forget a face like yours. But I can't for the life of me think where."

She laughed lightly for what else could she do. They were not touching but they were both aware of each other, senses heightened, and she should go now before it was too late. At her side she heard him catch his breath, wondered if she had done the same.

Time stood still and neither of them moved.

"What are we going to do?" he whispered. "What are you and I going to do, Vanessa my sweetheart?"

"Do?" she asked, stunned by the endearment. Had he really said that? "What do you mean?"

"We can admit how we feel about each other to each other," he said, voice low, for the deck of a Nile steamer where sound was apt to carry was not the best place to have a conversation such as this. "Ever since we met I've thought of nobody but you. I told you why I married Kathleen…"

"Yes, you did tell me."

"Believe me, I would never have agreed to get married if I didn't feel something for Kathleen. She is the sweetest girl but if I had met you first, if you hadn't already been married to Theodore then I would have married you, Vanessa. Because I love you and you love me. Don't you?"

She looked at him then and even though she said not a word, she answered the question in her eyes.

"It's too late," she said in an agonized whisper. "You must see that. I like Kathleen and I would do nothing to upset her. And I admire Theodore greatly. I am sorry, William, but it is just impossible."

She moved away but, with a little groan, he caught her hand, pulling her back to him with a single movement.

"Please, don't do this," she muttered, making a vain attempt to escape his grasp but he was too strong and his smile was much too sweet and she loved him anyway and it was taking all her strength not to give in at this moment, to melt against him, to have him kiss her at last.

"Why is it too late? What can be wrong when we love each other as we do? I have to see you again, Vanessa. I can't say goodbye forever." He turned her face to his, ran a finger over her mouth, all the while looking deeply into her eyes. "You are so breathtakingly beautiful."

He was closing in on her, their bodies pressed together, and she could have made some effort then but, mesmerised by his nearness, she did not and, at last, he kissed her. She wound her arms up round his neck and their mutual delight was such, instant and sparkling, that the kisses would have continued if they had been anywhere but here, on deck, dangerously in full view. All too soon, mindful of their situation, he pulled away and they stood there, hands back on the rail, inches apart, shaking with emotion, unable to speak, not daring now to look at each other. After all this time, after the years of dreaming, it had finally happened. William loved her. She would cherish this kiss to her dying day.

"I'm sorry," he said at last. "That was unforgiveable of me. I always thought of myself as an honourable man and Kathleen is my bride. She loves me and I must take care of her for she is not strong. I will never leave her."

"And I will never leave Theodore. I would never hurt him." She bit her lip, still reeling. "It might be best if we don't see each other again up in Lancashire."

"Of course." He gave a short laugh. "We must make sure of that. But why, oh why, didn't I meet you before now? You are the love of my life, Vanessa, and always will be but it's not to be."

Out of the corner of her eye, Vanessa thought she caught a flash of burnt orange, the same colour as the gown Lady Palmer was wearing for the last musical soiree. She watched that lady anxiously later but there was no trace in her demeanour that she had witnessed anything untoward and she remembered that the lady was short sighted but far too vain to do anything about it.

Kathleen was recovered by the time dinner was served, her smile as bright and her manner as charming as ever, her skin and hair flattered by the soft mint green gown, dancing every dance with her husband and as Vanessa watched them whirl by she felt such strong guilt that she wished the floor would swallow her up.

CHAPTER EIGHT

Standing at her bedroom window of the Asher house in Chelsea, Vanessa looked out onto the leafy square, the leaves turning now as autumn approached. The smell was fresh after a shower of rain. She loved the English weather with all its variations and it was so welcome after the heat of Egypt, the memory of which was now fading.

Theodore was increasingly preoccupied, shutting himself away in his library and leaving her to spend the evenings alone, listening to the wireless, reading or sewing.

And now, against all odds, she was pregnant. She knew that Theodore and Henrietta would be delighted. It was hard to believe that the lukewarm lovemaking in the French hotel on the journey home with Teddy mildly intoxicated might have produced a baby but it had.

She would choose the right moment to tell him. Good news was in short supply these days with everybody getting twitchy about a possible war. Theodore was now a member of the Architectural Association, a prominent and successful businessman but he allowed his mother to influence him still and she was always getting him involved with dubious ventures overseas. It was a worry. Vanessa had tried to warn him about the latest one, certain that it would lead him into trouble but been soundly rebuffed for her efforts.

She sighed, turning away from the window.

"Would you get me a glass of water, please Annie?"

It was a large house and they employed a core staff which Theodore was talking of reducing. Occasionally, he had an attack of conscience about their extravagances, which was laughable because it was he who had insisted on their exotic holiday. Theodore spent a fortune on clothes, a well dressed man to the point of fanaticism. Theodore would hang himself rather than go out to a function improperly clad and he was very generous towards Vanessa.

"Water, Mrs Asher..."

"Thank you, Annie." Thankfully, she raised her head and sipped the water. "I felt a little faint and nauseous. I can't think why..." she stopped, as she saw the knowing look on the girl's face, a young girl who had no less than nine brothers and sisters.

"I'm told ginger biscuits are very good for taking the edge off it, madam," Annie said, her cheeks even brighter than usual. "My mum swears by them."

Vanessa dismissed her with a nod and the girl scurried out.

She must tell Theodore at once before he heard about it from the servants. It made her smile as she remembered that her mum had known all there was to know about the Whitlocks and how the kitchen at Ruby House had been a hive of gossip. The servants' grapevine was assured and she might as well have placed an announcement in the Times for it would be all around town by tomorrow that the mistress was in the family way.

***

In spite of Teddy's disapproval of Mrs Crawford and what he called her activities, Vanessa continued to visit occasionally although she was wise enough to rarely mention it to her husband.

They felt a little like duty visits for Vanessa still worried about her association with the lady, aware that Mrs Crawford, like Tony Walsh, could wreck everything if she chose.

Today, Mrs Flintoff was paying a visit and the two ladies expressed joy at Vanessa's news and, for a while, Mrs Flintoff talked of her own family matters before moving on to what seemed to be her current favourite subject; the gradual demise of George Whitlock.

"Poor Martha is having a dreadful time with him," she said. "I am afraid he is…" she lowered her voice to a whisper and they craned forward. "… losing his mind, poor man." She continued after a respectful pause. "He is becoming very forgetful lately and that is a sad fact that the family wish to keep private so you must be discreet, Florence. I promised Martha I would not say a word about it to anyone although as you live here in London that hardly counts. He insists she read a chapter of a book every evening because his eyesight is failing. She is dredging through "King Solomon's Mines" just now and so bored with it."

"How sad," Mrs Crawford murmured. "He was always such an energetic gentleman too. I believe the workforce thought highly of him."

"Quite so. As to William's wife…" she sniffed. "Kathleen Winstanley may hail from a good Lancashire family but she is such a silly girl and delicate too. I can't think what they were thinking of in deciding that she would be a suitable match. There's no sign of a baby for her yet," she said, nodding towards Vanessa whose figure as yet betrayed no signs of pregnancy. "They do say she has fits. I always feel ginger-haired ladies are at a disadvantage. They never seem robust creatures to me."

"Vanessa tells me that Mrs Whitlock was sickly on the river cruise in Egypt." Mrs Crawford said.

"It was the heat," Vanessa pointed out. "It was stifling at times and she was overcome by it."

"Of course." Mrs Flintoff nodded thoughtfully. "I had forgotten you met them. How awful for you under the circumstances to meet somebody from Preston although you have made such a successful transformation one would never guess your humble background. Your accent is impeccable, my dear." She and Mrs Crawford exchanged a quick glance, these two ladies who knew her secret. It occurred that too many people knew her secret and it would only take one of them to unmask her. It was an uncomfortable feeling but she dismissed it as a silly notion. It was being pregnant that did it. It was making her feel extra vulnerable. "How did you find her?" Mrs Flintoff switched on an insincere smile. "The new Mrs Whitlock?"

"She is charming," Vanessa said, aware that anything she said might find its way back to Kathleen for she did not trust Mrs Flintoff one little bit. "As I say, she found the heat exhausting but then we all did."

She regretted now telling Mrs Crawford about meeting up with the Whitlocks but she had just blurted it out the first time she saw her once she had returned home.

She did not of course mention the kiss.

***

Snape Hall was in a class of its own. Vanessa found it gloomy, cold and uninspiring, its stone the dark murky grey of a troubled sky. It was beloved of Henrietta's family, however, and as such there were no plans to disown it or sell it so Vanessa had little option but to take up the mantle of trying to improve it and bring it up to date.

Theodore was generous with a budget to buy some new furniture and soft furnishings and Vanessa knew she would have to brave a trip into Preston to look at a selection of items.

Kathleen Whitlock at least loved the house. To Vanessa's dismay, Theodore insisted on extending a weekend invitation to the Whitlock's some time after they were back and she had been unable to think of a good enough excuse not to invite them without arousing his suspicions. She was annoyed with William for accepting it but realised that not accepting the invitation might be seen as a slur and not in the best business interests.

"What a glorious house and what lovely views. Do you know that you can see the Isle of Man and your Welsh mountains on a clear day from the top of Longridge Fell?" Kathleen said as the two of them took tea in the drawing room.

"I didn't know," she murmured, half smiling at the reference to her Welsh mountains. She no longer worried about Kathleen asking awkward questions for by now she was much more adept at dealing with them.

"You are so lucky to be able to escape London. I want William to buy a country house," she told Vanessa. The men were in the library talking business and the ladies were taking afternoon tea. "I'm so glad you asked us over. You must forgive me but I've been so very busy that I haven't been able to give a thought to entertaining. It's very remiss of me and my sister-in-law Martha is cross with me for certain people expect an invitation. I am afraid Martha's taste in furnishings is so old-fashioned so I need to buy new curtains and cushions and things. We could go shopping together sometime if you like."

"That would be lovely and don't worry yet about entertaining. I'm sure people will give you more time to get settled in properly," Vanessa said, wondering if Kathleen would always have this effect of making her feel like an older much wiser sister.

"I hope so but you haven't met Martha who is getting very cross with me. Aren't families difficult?" Kathleen said, letting out a huge sigh. "Do you get on with Theodore's mother?"

"Very well." Vanessa smiled. She liked Kathleen but she knew better than to criticize her mother-in-law. "Mama is a wonderful lady," she added, hoping that Kathleen did not detect sarcasm for the truth was Henrietta was difficult to please although, now she was pregnant, things were easier.

It seemed Kathleen had no such qualms in talking about her own family. "My father-in-law is driving us mad these days and acting very oddly. He is always going on about his will. He changes it week by week as the fancy takes him. As it stands, he is leaving the lot to William…" she grimaced, her indiscretion knowing no bounds. "Martha doesn't mind because she has the house in the country and a private income but the bulk of the fortune and the business goes to William until his son arrives that is and then a chunk will go to him when he is of age. We are instructed to call our son George William which is such a shame because I love the name Ashley for a boy. Don't you?"

"I do." She smiled a little. "Although it doesn't go with Asher so I shan't choose it for my son."

"Ashley Asher…" Kathleen giggled. "Anyway, father-in-law keeps looking at me waiting for the announcement. Isn't that appalling?"

"Disconcerting I should think."

"Absolutely. But the thing is…" she gave a little excited shrug. "Can you keep a secret? I think I may be expecting."

"Congratulations. That is good news." Vanessa smiled although for a moment the news had hit her hard. Of course William would father a child by Kathleen for they were husband and wife but she still didn't want him to and was ashamed of the thought. "How exciting."

"Yes, isn't it? And, if I am expecting, and I'm not quite sure yet, our babies will be born not too far apart. Do you want a boy?" she asked, taking a glance towards Vanessa's now obvious bump.

"Yes, I do. And a daughter next time."

Kathleen grimaced. "I don't know if there will be a next time for me if it's a boy. I'm not very strong and I don't like babies much."

"But you'll love your own baby," Vanessa reassured her. "That's quite different. I'm nervous myself."

"Are you? You seem very composed to me."

"Do I? I don't feel it."

"It's probably because we don't know what to expect. Oh please don't say anything to anybody yet. After all, I'm not sure," she paused, flushed. "Sorry. I shouldn't speak of such things, not over tea."

"Do have a piece of cake." Vanessa said, by way of changing the subject.

"Thank you. Did I tell you that William's taken over at the mill now?"

"Oh. That is good."

"He is determined to have much better cooperation with the workers and the union and make things a lot safer for them which will involve spending a lot of money on new machinery."

"That's very commendable."

"I suppose so but honestly what do they expect? I think William should be careful not to spend too much. My father-in-law maintains that the machines will last for another twenty years saving a huge amount of money."

"What does William say to that?"

"Gracious, I have no idea." she gave another girlish giggle. "We only speak occasionally about his work for he knows how it bores me. Martha insists on telling me things for she says I should have some knowledge of it. It is quite a dangerous place, Vanessa, and I am afraid there are bound to be little accidents from time to time, the weavers getting their sleeves caught, the mule spinners slipping on the floor breaking a leg, that sort of thing."

Vanessa was surprised she knew about mule spinners. One of her neighbours had been one and the humid atmosphere had done for his chest. He worked bare foot to reduce the danger of slipping on that oily floor and, according to his wife, his feet were terrible to behold.

"Accidents happen," Kathleen went on cheerfully. "But it's rarely anything serious."

"That's comforting to know."

A cold air had escaped into the room despite the fire in the hearth, and Vanessa let loose a sigh. She recalled the cotton dust that seemed to settle in a permanent haze round her old neighbours and the coughs it caused.

Oblivious to Vanessa's thoughts, Kathleen continued. "I expect I shall have to pay a visit to the weaving shed soon because that's what Martha used to do and she says it encourages the workers. I am to help organize the works outing too and make up little presents for them to take on the charabanc and then stand there in the yard and wave them goodbye." She pulled a face. "Martha is very keen on such things. She says you have to show the workers that you care for them."

"And do you? Care for them?" Vanessa asked.

Again, Kathleen seemed not to notice the sharp tone, simply shrugging the question away.

"There have been a couple of dreadful accidents…" she went on, leaning forward, eyes aglow. "Years ago a man was almost decapitated by a flying shuttle. Apparently, the men gathered round at once so that the women could not see but there was blood simply everywhere. He died on the spot," she finished, wiping cream off her finger.

"What was his name?" Vanessa asked, picking up the teapot and pouring tea with a steady hand.

"Name?" Kathleen seemed astonished at the question. "I don't know. Harry somebody I believe. It was a big story at the time, the first fatality in the mill. Did you read of it in the paper in London?"

"I must have." Vanessa replaced the silver pot on the tray.

"My father-in-law frets about it because he knew the shuttles were loose and long overdue being replaced for the union man complained about them just days before it happened," she went on, a tiny spot of cream sticking to the corner of her mouth. "So, ridiculously, my father-in-law has started to blame himself when he was completely cleared at the inquest. He keeps going on and on about it these days. The man, Harry somebody, was a bully and was disliked although of course nobody wished an end like that for him. There was quite a to-do following the inquest verdict. The wife caused a scene and then as he passed by she spat at Mr Whitlock," she added with distaste. "Imagine that? His coat was ruined by spittle. And then, do you know, she died herself weeks later. Of a broken heart so they say. I ask you..." she laughed. "What a notion. How could somebody like that die of a broken heart? They have no feelings, people like that. How can they have? They have no education. Some of them can't even read or write. Sadly, they are born into poverty and die in it but we do our best to make life bearable for them." She reached for another tiny cake. "I shouldn't be talking of such unpleasant things, not to a lady in your condition. I am so sorry. Forgive me."

"Sugar?" Vanessa pushed the bowl of lump sugar and the tongs towards her, wishing they were pellets of arsenic.

CHAPTER NINE

Next morning Vanessa found herself alone in the morning room with William. The maid was dismissed and they dallied over toast and marmalade and tea.

"I thought we agreed that we would not see each other again," William said. "So, why did you invite us here? I would have refused the invitation but Kathleen told Martha and that was the end of it. My sister wants us to widen our circle of friends and was quite excited at the prospect so it became impossible to refuse," he said, voice low.

"It was Theodore's doing," she said, daring at last to meet his eyes. She was wearing a simple pale blue day dress, loose to allow for her pregnancy, and very little make-up and she did not feel anywhere near her best but his gaze now they were alone was still full of admiration. "He was insistent and I could not think of a reason why we should not invite you. I am so sorry." She fiddled with her napkin, avoiding stretching out her hand because she worried he might take hold of it. "I... about that evening, William..."

"Let's blame it on that glorious sunset," he said. "And let's say no more about it."

She nodded.

"Congratulations on your news," he went on. "Kathleen and I are delighted for you both. You will be a good mother."

"I hope so," she said, allowing herself a little frisson of joy as she thought of the child growing within her. "Theodore is very pleased. As you will be when Kathleen has a child. She let me into a little secret yesterday…"

"She is not expecting," he interrupted her. "She thought she was but she's not. She is not strong and I worry that she is too delicate to carry a child. Occasionally, she has little episodes. She's suffered from them all her life and the doctor is concerned about her health. So, even though my father is desperate for her to have a child to carry on the Whitlock name, I ask myself how can I put her through it if there is the slightest danger to her life?"

She saw the concern in his face and knew then if she didn't know before, that this man was fond of his wife and would never do anything to hurt her.

And that was exactly as it should be.

Their love, the passionate love they felt for each other, was doomed from the start, a silly dream on her part that she could not seem to be able to squash but it was a relief to her that, alone now, they were able to conduct themselves in so convivial and controlled a manner. There would be no more kisses.

"Goodness, look at the time. If you'll excuse me, William…" she rose from the table, glad that her face was hidden from his eyes as she headed for the door for, emotionally overloaded as she was in her present state, she could barely hold back her tears.

***

Charles Aloysius Theodore Asher was a plump healthy baby with dimpled cheeks, dark-haired like his mother, and, to her, the most beautiful baby ever.

She adored him from the first moment she saw him. As he grew older, she could see her sister Maggie in him, in that straight gaze from wise eyes. She was pleased with Betty, the girl she engaged, Theodore happy to leave that appointment to her. He had seen the war coming and they listened to the broadcast back in September in silence. He got up and switched off the wireless, standing there a minute, head bowed.

"My God," he said. "I was right but I take no pleasure in that. It's a mess, my dear, but we shall get through it."

Vanessa rushed to look out of the window, stupidly worried that there might be a German plane flying over at that very moment ready to drop its bombs.

It was a poor time to bring a child into the world. The war brought businesses to their knees and worryingly some of Theodore's contracts ground to a halt through lack of investors, his grandiose plans for a chain of picture houses going back into the desk drawer. He had shown the sketches to her and she had been excited to see them. They rarely went to the pictures themselves, more often to the theatre now, but she recalled those picture-going days with affection.

Every evening without fail, she went to the nursery to spend time with her baby whilst Theodore removed himself to his study to write letters. Betty would disappear and Vanessa sat Charles on her knee, talking to him, seeing his sometimes serious little face absorbing her words. She wished she could spend more time with him but in her position it was impossible. She had to leave the daily tasks to Betty who did it well for Charles was always presented to her sweet smelling and prettily clothed.

Times like this she thought often of Lizzie who would have loved to hold her baby.

"Auntie Lizzie is our secret," she murmured to Charles, settling him into her arms and kissing the top of his baby-fine hair as he drifted off to sleep.

Her son would have the best of everything.

For him, she would do anything to ensure that he had a proper place in society when he grew up.

For him, she would allow Theodore to dispatch him off to school when he was eight so that he might have the best education.

For him, she would continue to suppress her roots and as he grew and became aware she would cease to talk to him about Lizzie.

Theodore was moving Vanessa and Charles up north for the duration of the war. It was a nuisance but Vanessa, a little scared, had to admit that Theodore was right. Unknown to Theodore who obeyed Government instructions to the letter, she had laid in a supply of silk stockings - heaven forbid that she should run out - and she had an ample supply of her favourite "Je Reviens", although she would have to use it sparingly from now on.

***

After a long silence, there was a note from Mrs Crawford, enquiring as to her health. Feeling guilty, Vanessa wrote her a lengthy letter in reply. It wasn't just that Teddy disapproved of Mrs Crawford for the truth was that she herself wanted to draw a line under her arrival in London. But she had to remember that Mrs Crawford was privy to her secret and was still in occasional contact with her mother-in-law Henrietta so it was with something of a heavy heart that she contacted her, suggesting they meet for one of the lunchtime concerts at The National Gallery.

Vanessa went alone. Although Mrs Crawford was disappointed not to see Charles, she understood the difficulty and perhaps after all, a lunchtime recital listening to Bach was hardly the right place for a baby boy who could be fretful at times.

They found a quiet corner, music in the background, where they were able to conduct a lowly voiced conversation.

"You look well, my dear," Mrs Crawford said, studying her. "You wear that lavender colour well too. It becomes you. In fact, I am pleased to see that you have developed such a stylish mode of dress. I wish I could be more adventurous but I am quite settled with grey."

"Have you heard from Mrs Flintoff recently?"

"Oh yes. She and I keep up a regular correspondence," she said. "Mr Crawford has a new lady now. One of his shop girls," she added with a sniff. "It never works that sort of thing. You have to stick to your kind."

"But…"

"I didn't mean you of course, Vanessa. You and Theodore are wonderfully suited to each other. Does he make you happy?"

She nodded, not wanting to go into details.

"And William Whitlock?" She smiled. "I take it, that's all in the past, that stupid infatuation you had with the man. I expect seeing him afresh has dampened those feelings."

"Yes. He is happily married as am I," she said firmly.

"I have news of them. My dear, I know you will be interested to know that Kathleen Whitlock is expecting. She is not well so it is worrying."

"I am sorry to hear that although I am pleased to hear about the baby," Vanessa said and surprisingly she was. "She will have the best of care. I am sure she will be fine."

"I am not so sure. She has the look of a woman who will not live long. It is worrying enough having a baby without this war going on at the same time although it will help that William's work will mean he stays at home." She shot a glance at

Vanessa. "Henrietta tells me that Theodore is to be engaged with war work of a specific nature. Do you know anything about that?"

She shook her head. It seemed sometimes that Theodore discussed important things more with Henrietta than her. It was as if they were both trying to protect her from bad news. It was mad because if they knew her real background, they would know that she had a strength within her that could cope with anything life could throw at her. However, it suited her that they should dismiss her thus for Mrs Crawford was right. Having strong opinions in her situation was a very bad idea.

"Do you hear any news of Lizzie?" she asked deciding a change of subject was necessary.

"According to Mrs Flintoff, Lizzie has moved to a little house in Tithebarn Street."

Vanessa frowned. Lizzie would be middle aged now but, unless she had improved greatly, she doubted she could look after herself properly.

"She manages," Mrs Crawford said, reading her mind. "Her neighbour is a kindly lady and helps all she can. Lizzie sews and takes in ironing."

"Good."

"You worry about her too much. She never concerned herself with your welfare, did she? Apparently, she told the neighbour that she was all alone in the world, an orphan without any siblings." Mrs Crawford raised her eyebrows. "She's forgotten you, my dear, as you must forget her. I told you to do that years ago and I am disappointed that you still talk of her."

As they said goodbye, Mrs Crawford kissed her, absentmindedly calling her Nessa. It was the first time she had been called that in years and it sounded odd and was a concern if Mrs Crawford of all people was becoming careless.

***

Snape Hall, as well as its gardens, was going to seed. The couple who were caretaking, the Barkers, did their best but it was a huge house and required a huge staff and the young men, including their own son, were gone away. They were a stoic couple, the Barkers, and, before he left, their son Eddie had got married to a lovely girl called Eleanor.

Hearing about the impending nuptials, Vanessa lent Mrs Barker one of her suits, a deep burgundy one, and that lady was everlastingly grateful for that.

"He might never come home," she told Vanessa sadly, on the eve of the wedding. "But Eleanor won't have that. She says she will wait for him but they wanted to be married first, to have some time together. I just hope she doesn't get in the family way, not straight off although it would give her something to remember him by, wouldn't it, if he doesn't come back?"

"Come on, Mrs Barker, don't say things like that. Eddie will be back," Vanessa told her, thinking that she seemed to spend all her time these days consoling people but somebody had to stay optimistic or they would all sink into gloom.

She attended the ceremony, in a deliberately buoyant mood for people took note of her these days, wearing a jaunty straw trilby hat with a pheasant feather, and, seeing the two young people standing at the altar, her heart had ached for them. It was plain for all to see that they adored each other and everybody must surely be thinking the same thing. Would he come back to her or would he be killed in some foreign field before long?

She thought of her own wedding, standing beside Theodore, catching a glimpse on the way up the aisle of Mrs Crawford, an anxious looking Mrs Crawford. She spoke her required lines perfectly, beautifully, not really listening to the words themselves but concentrating purely on the way she said them. Like an actress on stage, she had been utterly convincing to the extent of convincing herself. Looking back, she knew that she had never loved Theodore, not truly, but her hopes that things would work out had been very strong that day.

And now, years later, at the wedding of Eddie and Eleanor, she stood outside the church with the other guests as the photographer, hidden under a black velvet cloth, urged them all to smile.

"Forget the bloody war, for God's sake, smile," he yelled and smile they did.

***

"Mr Barker is driving me over to Preston this afternoon," she told Betty, catching her as she strolled with Charles in his pram, giving him his daily dose of fresh cold air. It was crisp underfoot and first thing the grounds had been covered in a hard frost.

Would this war ever get started? People were calling it the phoney war for nothing much was happening as if Hitler had been caught unawares and the expected air-raids had not materialised. She had asked Theodore if she and Charles might return to London but he refused saying, once it got going, London would be badly hit.

She knew they were to think carefully before using the car, Theodore's beloved Bentley, but if she stayed cooped up here a moment longer she would scream. "I am taking tea with Mrs William Whitlock at Ruby House in Preston," she explained to Betty although there was of course no need to offer an explanation. She was mistress of the house and she could do whatever she wanted, whenever she wanted.

"Very good, madam." Betty bobbed her head. Betty was not blessed with good looks with a pinched face, sharp nose and mousey hair. She had a soft voice though and it was one that often comforted her dearest Charles.

"How is my darling boy?"

"He had a bad night," Betty admitted, looking tired now that Vanessa looked closely at her. "He was hot and I had to sing to him to get him off. He likes Twinkle Twinkle Little Star best. He was very fretful but after I gave him a Fennings powder he cooled down but I am keeping an eye on him just in case."

Vanessa felt a moment's alarm but she was confident of Betty's ability to know the difference between teething problems and serious illness. Betty adored her son and she trusted her implicitly.

Betty pulled back the baby's covers so that Vanessa could see him properly. Poor Charles was not at his best with one flushed cheek but, as she smiled down at him, he smiled back showing two front teeth, a little dribble of milk at the corner of his mouth. He looked so like her and she felt anew that sharp pain of love. With his hair thickening, curling and darkening, Charles was developing a look of her own father and his sometimes sly look reminded her uncomfortably of Lizzie.

He had the Asher chin though.

CHAPTER TEN

"Here we are, madam," Barker said, drawing the car to a halt outside the house.

"Thank you." She was in no rush to get out but Barker nipped out smartly to open her door and she had no time to collect herself together. She had not been in this area for ages and, looking out of the car window on the way here, it was as if she could glimpse the ghost of the girl she had once been for it had changed little over the years. She had been so proud of her dress, Lizzie's dress, but she had let herself down by wearing the lipstick and being in a dream during the interview.

No more cold stone servants' steps for her, not now, but her mouth felt dry as she walked up to the front door. Every now and then she felt as if she was just a step away from being found out.

She ought not to be here.

She did not deserve to be here.

Wearing a dark green coat with a Persian lamb collar over a paler green dress, Vanessa stepped into Ruby House through the front door. Having been relieved of her coat, hat and gloves by a maid she was ushered into the drawing room where Kathleen was waiting. She had received several invitations from the lady for afternoon tea but had managed to find excuses but they had now run out and here she was.

"It's so lovely to see you again," her hostess said. "And how well you look."

"Thank you. You look very well too," she said, although it was not quite true for Kathleen looked as if she had lost weight which she could ill afford.

"I am as well as can be expected," Kathleen said with a small smile. "How is life up here for you?"

"It's quiet but peaceful and safer for Charles. I would prefer to be with Theodore but he was quite insistent that we remove ourselves."

"Children are being evacuated I hear, poor little souls. I was in London a few weeks ago. I found it much changed but what can you expect?" Kathleen said, dark shadows under her eyes indicating that she was not sleeping well. "I stayed at Claridge's and the guests were trying to behave as normal although everybody is on edge. I think some ladies are in denial about the situation but they are stocking up on supplies nonetheless."

"Theodore gets very cross about that," Vanessa said. "But I must confess I have more than enough silk stockings tucked away and, in any case, it should all be over by Christmas."

They shared a smile.

"I visited Lady Edith Palmer whilst I was there," Kathleen said. "Do you remember her?"

"Of course. How could I forget? How is she?"

"Ailing, I'm afraid. She asked me to visit because she needed to tell me something before her health fails completely. Something has been on her conscience for some time." She waved a hand. "Do sit down, Vanessa. Tea will be along in a moment. Isn't winter a hard time? The trees look so bare and we have few flowers just now. When the war is over, I shall fill the beds with roses and cast the vegetables aside. They are nowhere near as pretty."

Vanessa settled down and smiled, aware though of a strained atmosphere. For a while, they talked of the weather and the garden, pausing as a maid arrived with the tea tray, resuming the conversation when she had departed. Kathleen poured the tea but she was not a skilled hostess, in spite of the finishing school, falling uncomfortably silent so that it was left to Vanessa to jolly things along.

"When do you expect the baby?" she asked.

"In summer." After dispensing the tea, Kathleen lowered herself into a chair, slowly as if she were an old lady, raising her feet onto a footstool. "My ankles are swelling already and I have been so sick, keeping nothing down. How can the child inside me be thriving?"

"They do," Vanessa said. "They make very sure they take all they need from you. Unfortunately, it can mean that you feel poorly but it gets better until the last month when it becomes a chore just moving about." She smiled. "Sorry, I'm sure you don't want to hear that. I was enormous but then Charles was a good weight."

"My baby will not be. I fear the child will be born prematurely and die and I with it. I am so frightened, Vanessa."

"Good heavens, Kathleen, what are you talking about?" Vanessa sat up straight. "My experience with Charles was nowhere near as bad as they make out."

It was a blatant lie but a necessary one in order to calm poor Kathleen. She remembered Lizzie telling her about her own mother screaming the house down when she arrived in the world and feared she had done the same. Charles was born in the bedroom of the London house and, through the haze of pain, she recalled that her new manner of speaking completely deserted her and she reverted to her Lancastrian roots. It had been an uncomplicated birth at that without the need for the doctor's assistance. She hoped she could rely on the midwife's discretion for it must have been a surprise to her to hear her, a supposed lady, ranting like a fishwife.

"We are all the same, madam, princess or pauper, when it comes to pushing out a babe," the midwife had said matter-of-factly when it was blessedly over. "We all take on in different ways and you were very brave."

"But some of the things I said..." she murmured, trying to recall them.

"I never listened. I had my job to do," the midwife fussed around her. "And they wouldn't have heard down below stairs either and I made sure nobody was outside on the landing. Now, if you're ready, I'll go and break the news to everybody. I know Mr Asher is waiting patiently at the end of the telephone and I shall tell him he has a fine healthy boy, an eight pounder at that."

Theodore, so far as she knew, had spent the day at his Club, returning to find her lying in bed amongst clean sheets wearing a crisp new nightgown with her hair brushed and baby Charles swaddled in his cot. She remembered him taking a cursory glance at the baby, nodding and pronouncing him a fine fellow before coming to her and kissing her on the cheek and telling her yet again that she had done very well. Henrietta visited promptly, overjoyed, although she did not go so far as to pick up the child.

Duty done then so far as Henrietta and Theodore were concerned but one day she would repeat the process she hoped so that dearest Charles had a brother or sister.

"Ladies try to scare you when you are expecting," she told Kathleen now, seeing the fear in her eyes. "You really must not believe a word of it. When it's happening to you, it's perfectly bearable."

"You are telling the truth, Vanessa?" Kathleen shuddered. "My mama says childbirth is quite dreadful. She is going to pray for me."

"You forget the whole business the minute the child is placed in your arms," Vanessa assured her and that, at least, was true.

"At least my condition spares me from doing anything for the war effort," Kathleen continued with a wry smile. "Martha is quite in her element. She's very patriotic and I believe she has been waiting for this moment for years. At last she has an excuse to boss everybody about in the WVS. She says some of the women are still acting as if they are at a cocktail party playing at charades. She says she cannot see any of them being of the slightest use in an emergency, not if it means they might tear their very last pair of stockings. Won't it be a bore if we end up short of essentials such as that? What on earth will we do?"

"We won't run out of things. People love to spread rumours."

"Please don't treat me like a child and try to humour me. William does it all the time," Kathleen said softly, surprising her. "Things will only get worse, believe me. We are a sitting target here with the docks and William is concerned about the mill. I am going to stay with my mother in Lytham and have the baby there. It should be safer."

Vanessa nodded, at a loss as to how to proceed for Kathleen seemed determined in her melancholy, sighing as she offered her a piece of cake; an eggless, fatless walnut cake entirely devoid of flavour.

"How is William?" she asked. "Well, I trust?"

"Oh yes, he is well. It is kind of you to enquire after him."

Vanessa nibbled at the cake but she was in such turmoil that she might as well have been eating sawdust. It was bad enough sitting here in the drawing room of Ruby House without Kathleen behaving so oddly. Even allowing for her pregnancy and her concern over that, she seemed different, older somehow, and Vanessa sensed that she was working up to something.

But what? A little sliver of alarm passed through her for, despite the polite smiles, the inconsequential chat, something was not quite right. The mention of Lady Palmer had caused her to reflect once more on that night and a sudden premonition of doom circled her, Kathleen's next words not helping.

"You haven't brought the child with you?" her voice was sharp. "I did ask you to."

"Charles is a little fretful. I am sorry but it was better to leave him at home."

"Is that the only reason?"

Vanessa paused. "What do you mean?" she asked carefully for the question had a hard edge to it that she could not fail to notice.

"I hear he does not favour his father in appearance. Lady Palmer has an acquaintance who knows your mother-in-law and she says as much. She says baby Charles resembles you," Kathleen said and now with the pretences gone you could cut the atmosphere of the room with a knife. "I am not a complete fool, Vanessa, and I can do sums. I know how long it takes to make a baby and I can count back nine months to our cruise. Lady Palmer was on deck that last night and so were you and my husband."

The cold glare spoke volumes. Swallowing the last of the dreadful cake, Vanessa wondered how she would get out of this.

***

The tea party was abruptly ended at that point for Kathleen was taken ill, her plate and cake sliding off her knee and, as Vanessa went to her aid, she saw to her horror that her eyes were rolling about in her head and that there was a thin layer of perspiration on her forehead. She was making little jittery movements too that scared Vanessa who had never coped well with medical matters.

She called for help and Kathleen's maid was there in a trice, pushing Vanessa aside whilst she administered to her mistress and Vanessa wisely took her leave.

***

Vanessa had no idea what to do about Kathleen and the accusation.

She did telephone the Whitlock residence the next day, politeness demanding it, to enquire after the lady's health and was told that madam was recovered but unable to come to the telephone.

Would she keep quiet? As Kathleen had been taken ill immediately after she had uttered the words, they had no time to discuss it, an accusation that she would have strenuously denied. She could not deny the kiss for that had been witnessed by that busybody Lady Palmer but she could have passed it off as a momentary aberration.

There was no need for Kathleen to know that she had harboured deep feelings for William for years, that he featured often in her dreams, that sometimes on the few occasions Theodore and she made love, she imagined it to be William.

That was a shameful secret she held close.

In the meantime, all she could do was hope that Kathleen would not take this further. If Lady Palmer had blabbed to her then who else was in on the secret? It was surely only a matter of time before Theodore found out but, if he did, she felt sure she could talk him round. He adored her and she would plead a woman's innocence, even if it meant casting William in a poor light.

William would understand the dilemma she faced and she knew he had no wish to see her marriage disintegrate. A little mollified because she had some sort of plan she could call upon, she tried her best to settle into the life at Snape Hall and the weeks turning into months passed uneventfully. She began to breathe a sigh of relief believing that it was forgotten, that Kathleen, soon to bring a child into the world, had no wish to stir things up.

But, in summer, she was recalled to London as Mrs Crawford wished to see her as a matter of urgency, something that could not be discussed over the telephone. She left Charles in Betty's charge telling her she would not be staying long.

"It's all right, madam, I shall look after him. Won't I, my little soldier?" Betty took him from Vanessa and he at once leaned into her, cuddled against her.

Vanessa felt a sharp pang of jealousy and irritation that he should do that. Did he prefer Betty? Surely not, yet Betty was the one who comforted him in the early hours if he was upset, not her.

He hardly knew Theodore either but that was not unusual in their world for fathers were often distant figures.

***

Mrs Crawford met her in the hall, Vanessa noting the worried look in her eyes at once.

"You mustn't be upset, my dear but you have a visitor. I know this is going to be a shock to you but try not to be too distressed."

"Who is it?"

"It's your sister Lizzie."

"Lizzie? But how did she get here? How did she know where you lived?"

"She won't say," Mrs Crawford said. "She refuses to tell me. I dread to think what might have happened to her on the way. I tried to ask but she said if a man tried to do anything to her, she'd murder him. She was carrying a knife in her pocket."

Vanessa nodded. The same old Lizzie.

Mrs Crawford looked closely at her. "Are you ready?"

"Yes..." she whispered, feeling quite ill.

Mrs Crawford reached over and rang a little bell and the door opened and Lizzie stood there, a Lizzie with greying hair and the same knowing eyes.

"Lizzie!" Vanessa turned her gaze at her sister. "I tried to keep in touch with you after Maggie died. I wrote letters to her but she never replied and then I wrote letters to be passed on to you but you never answered them either."

"Why should I? Hello, our Nessa."

Lizzie was now clean and tidy, courtesy of Mrs Crawford, but with a wild and sly look she remembered from long ago.

"I've been chucked out," she said tonelessly. "Nowhere to go. Nowt to live on. Except my wits," she added with that sudden odd smile. "What are you going to do about it?"

CHAPTER ELEVEN

Mrs Crawford left them and Lizzie came further into the room, walking in that splayed-out feet way of hers, eventually sitting down, fussing around, first on one chair and then another, her short legs dangling. She was wearing a homemade purple frock and a badly contrasting green knitted cardigan.

Vanessa, fingering her own elegant day dress with its padded shoulders and double breasted jacket, looked at her sister and could not help a little shake of her head.

"Somebody gave me a sewing machine and I made myself some new frocks from a Butterick pattern," Lizzie said, catching her gaze. "I'm good at sewing. I made a plain blue and a flowered. They are bonny frocks but I'm keeping them for best. This is all right, plenty of wear in it yet."

Vanessa nodded. "It's very nice," she said, feeling her smile taut on her face. "I have some dresses that might fit if you want to try them on?"

"Don't want your cast-offs. You used to wear my things once upon a time. Remember that? You once wore my best frock for that job you never got up at Ruby House. He's married now, that William Whitlock, to a lady with red hair. You were sweet on him, weren't you?"

"You have a good memory."

"I do." Lizzie grinned. "Maggie cried for days when you went. He laid into her too, something rotten. You shouldn't have left her."

"I wish I hadn't."

"She's dead. She took pneumonia."

"Yes, I know." Vanessa sighed. "Why didn't you reply to my letters, Lizzie? You could have got somebody to help you with them." She stopped because she had long suspected that the letters, her letters, had never been delivered, that it had been some elaborate deception by Mrs Crawford and Mrs Flintoff. The only news she ever had was by word of mouth from Mrs Flintoff and it distressed her beyond words that Maggie probably thought she had been forgotten. "You could have got somebody to help you write them," she went on, still half holding onto the pretence that they had not been torn up and put on Mrs Flintoff's fire.

"I don't need help. I can write letters myself." Lizzie drew herself up. "I didn't write because I had nowt to say. I've brought your letters with me."

Oh. So they were delivered. She offered up a silent apology to Mrs Flintoff.

"I've fastened a blue ribbon round them. They are my letters. Letters from my little sister in London." she finished proudly. "I've kept them all. Every single one."

"Oh, Lizzie..." the hurt in her chest shifted. "Did Maggie get letters from me?"

Lizzie nodded. "She picked them up from Peggy's shop and she said as she'd kill me if I told. She said it was too dangerous to keep them and she didn't want you getting into trouble. She threw them away. Tore them up into little bits before he got his hands on them although he wasn't so good at reading so likely he wouldn't have known what they were."

So Maggie had protected her at the last but why hadn't she replied? That would remain a mystery forever now.

"You got married, didn't you, just so you wouldn't be a spinster like me."

"I married Theodore because I fell in love with him," Vanessa told her, sounding totally unconvincing even to her own ears.

Lizzie laughed. "You did never, Nessa Cookson. You wed him for his money, more like. He's a real gent, Auntie Florence says."

"Mrs Crawford..." Vanessa corrected her absently. "You're not to call her Auntie Florence."

Lizzie shrugged. "Mrs Crawford then. You'll not be short of a bob or two then, our Nessa."

"And I'm Vanessa now."

"Not to me. What's the matter with Nessa? Nice name. Better than Lizzie. And that bangle was not real silver. I tried to sell it when I was hard up and they wouldn't even give me a tanner."

"It was a joke, Lizzie, me saying that. How could I afford a silver bangle?"

"You told me it was silver. And it looked like silver. It shone like silver. Never let it off my arm for years in case somebody nicked it. Told everybody it was solid silver too."

"I can get you a new one, a real silver one now."

"Don't want another one. I like this. I still have it," she added, pushing up her sleeve to reveal it.

"I can get you some money." Vanessa said. "I can get you enough to tide you over. You'll be better off back in Preston where you belong."

Lizzie sniffed and fiddled in a pocket for a handkerchief, blowing her nose with gusto. "I could make things bad for you, our Nessa. I could tell him who you really are, that gent you married. What would he say if he knew you were from a mill house in Preston?"

"Why would you want to do that, Lizzie?" she asked, thinking quickly. Theodore had more or less abandoned the house up in Lancashire, happy for the moment for her and Charles to live there, out of harm's way, so she could put Lizzie up there, find her something to do and swear her somehow to everlasting silence. It was risky but then with Lizzie everything was risky.

"Don't want to go up to Chipping," Lizzie said, when Vanessa mentioned the plan. "I don't like the country. It stinks. And I don't want to be your skivvy."

"Who said anything about that? And what would you do down here?" Vanessa asked helplessly.

"Auntie Florence says I can stay with her until I get on my feet. I can wash up and stuff. And she might teach me how to play the piano. I've always wanted to play the piano."

Vanessa nodded encouragingly although she very much doubted if Mrs Crawford would let Lizzie within clumsy-finger distance of her beloved piano.

"And you needn't think you've got rid of me. I'm still telling."

"Then tell..." Vanessa lost patience, stood up, snatched up her bag, irritated that, of all people, Lizzie was the one who without fail made her lose her temper. Attack and bluff was the best way to deal with Lizzie. "Come to my house, come with me now, and say what you want and I shall deny everything and let's see who my husband believes. He loves me, Lizzie, so he'll have you whipped for lying and then arrested. You'll be lucky if you don't end up in the asylum for lunatics. They'll put you in prison for it. You'll be slopping out and weeing into a tin bucket..."

Lizzie stared at her with suddenly frightened eyes.

"Now, here's something for you..." she dug into her handbag, fetched out some money. "I'll get you some more and then you'll have to leave me alone. And you must never come near me again. Is that quite clear?"

"Is that quite clear?" Lizzie mimicked, some of the old fire back in her eyes. "You talk posh, Nessa. And you look like a lady." She reached out, snatched the money and stuffed it into her pocket. "I'm an auntie, a real auntie. You had a little lad, didn't you? He's called Charlie isn't he?"

"Charles," Vanessa told her, "And you're to keep away from him too. I'm giving you this money because I'll not have you starve but that's it."

Lizzie slipped stealthily off her chair and in a few steps came close.

"Goodbye, my little sister..." she said, the words low and seething. "I shan't forget this. The way you want rid of me. I hoped you might let me stay at your house but..."

"You've refused to come up to Chipping so don't you dare say that. And hasn't Mrs Crawford said you can stay here a while," Vanessa said. "But, take my advice and go home to Preston. You won't like it down here. Not when the bombs start."

"Bombs can't hurt me," Lizzie said defiantly. "I've a charmed life. A gypsy told me once that I would live to be a hundred. You'll be dead before me."

"Oh, Lizzie, love, don't be like this..." she flicked away sudden sharp tears, wishing that Maggie was here now. "Let's be friends. Please... " she stretched out her arms. "Come here."

Lizzie looked at her, hard, and then danced away. "Let me see your baby," she asked. "You promised me that you would let me hold your baby before you went away. Do you remember that? And now you say you won't let me see him."

She was right. Vanessa remembered the promise as she looked at her sister who was now looking at her with a pleading look in her eyes. Oh dear, Lizzie was such a trial.

"Sorry I said that and of course you can see him," she said. "But he's up in Chipping, Lizzie, and you're down here. If you want to hold him, you'll have to come up."

"You're trying to trick me. I'm staying here," Lizzie said, frowning as she considered this. "It took me forever to get down here. I was nearly murdered. Would have been if I hadn't had this on me…" she grinned, pulling the small knife out of the pocket of the frock. "Don't go anywhere without this."

She would never change.

"I can handle her," Mrs Crawford whispered to Vanessa on her way out. "Poor deluded child. What a sorry state she was in when she arrived. I shall make sure she has some clean clothes and proper shoes."

"Thank you. Keep her indoors now." Vanessa instructed as she went down the steps outside. "I don't want her following me."

And, even though Mrs Crawford did promise that, she found herself looking over her shoulder more than once on the journey home.

***

"Come into the sitting room and sit down, Vanessa," Theodore said, waylaying her in the hall.

"I have something to say to you. But first of all, did you enjoy your visit to Mrs Crawford?"

The question seemed casual enough but she detected an unusual coolness in his manner. Slowly, she removed her hat, a beret with tassel, head averted so that she could give herself a moment to consider why he looked so angry. Whilst not going so far as to forbid her the visits, he disapproved of them but, because Henrietta firmly believed in the whole sorry business, he was in something of a dilemma as he hated to cross his mother.

Vanessa followed him into the drawing room and sat down in her favourite chair, moving a cushion that she herself had embroidered.

"Sit down, Teddy," she said with a frown. "What on earth is the matter?"

"This afternoon whilst you were out, I had a visit from an acquaintance of ours..." Theodore began, using his pompous voice, chest puffed out, as, instead of sitting down, he began to pace the room. "Celia Holland."

"Celia?" Vanessa had met the lady a few times but she remained a mere acquaintance. "Oh dear, I'm sorry I missed her but she made no mention that she was planning to visit."

"Be quiet. You misunderstand. She knew you were out. She was here to see me."

"To see you? What on earth for?"

He laughed but it was a bitter sound, devoid of humour. "She was quite beside herself but she had to tell me something that somebody else had told her because she felt it was her neighbourly duty to do so."

"Honestly, that is typical of her." Nervously, she tried a small smile on him. "What has she been saying? It wasn't about the Pearson contract, was it? That could be very awkward with her husband practically running the war office. I did warn you," she added. She was not a complete fool and had overheard some whispered conversations between Theodore and his mother recently.

"What do you know of that and how dare you accuse me of anything?" he roared and she jumped at the sound, for he very rarely raised his voice. "How dare you, Mrs Asher?"

Astonished that he should call her that, she was silenced. She was hardly thinking straight anyway after seeing Lizzie. If she and Theodore were to have a difficult conversation then she needed to be in a more controlled frame of mind. Now, she felt very much on the defensive. Her mild-mannered husband looked as if he was about to expire, flushed, veins bulging, eyes wild and even his tie was askew which was unthinkable.

"Sit down, darling," she said softly, thinking that, whatever it was, it would be better if he was more relaxed.

"You have made a fool of me," Theodore said, stopping his pacing and coming closer. "And I will not be made a fool of," he continued, a little spot of spittle forming on his chin and she was reminded of her father and the blaze in his eyes when his temper boiled. It was enough to make her recoil. "I have never had a woman make a cuckold of me. I have a reputation to uphold and I thought that you, my wife, had the greatest respect for me."

"I do," she said hastily. "I really don't know what you are talking about, Theodore. When have I made a fool of you?"

"A cuckold, I said. And that is worse. You have deceived me for a long time. In Egypt for example," he said and her heart pounded. "You had a liaison there with William Whitlock. Deny it if you will. Were you and he lovers?" he sat down suddenly, flushing an even deeper red.

She laughed lightly, putting a hand up to her throat and fingering her pearls. "What nonsense! Goodness gracious, he was on his honeymoon."

"I know. And did that stop you? I regret marrying you. You've deceived me from the moment we met. Celia Holland expressed grave doubts about your authenticity."

She recalled the occasional dinner party with Celia and her husband. They had always been an ordeal; Celia's sly questions that she thought she handled well, the sometimes raised eyebrows, the little glances Celia exchanged with her husband. She had always felt uncomfortable in the older woman's presence and perhaps there was a reason for that. She remembered telling Theodore how uncomfortable the woman made her feel and he had laughed saying that it was obvious that Mrs Holland was jealous of Vanessa's beauty.

Theodore was not laughing now. She saw that there was only one way to proceed and that was to go on the attack. After all, Theodore was not exactly enamoured with Celia Holland either.

"What is this nonsense? How have I deceived you? And I should take no notice of anything that woman says." She saw he was a little calmer, decided she had to change tack if she was to win him over. "William's wife is charming. Why would I try to break up a happy marriage when I am happily married myself?"

"Shut up, you whore," he said, looking down and slamming a fist into his hand. The words silenced her once more and, ridiculously, she wondered if they could be heard downstairs, if indeed they could be heard outside in the street.

"Theodore, do calm down, it's not good for you to get into a state like this. You'll take a turn," she bit her lip, frantically trying to think how to get out of this.

"Someone overheard you," he said wearily, sinking back in his chair, looking as if he had been pricked like a balloon. "So you can stop all this pretence. Someone saw you and William together on the deck of the boat. He was kissing you and you, madam, were putting up no resistance. It was like something out of one of your silly films. Lady Palmer was so shocked that she has kept quiet all this time but one afternoon last week she was a guest of Celia's and I believe Celia was going on about Charles, saying how like me he was and she felt I ought to be informed. Lady Palmer didn't want to make mischief, merely to acquaint me with the facts."

"Hah! Of course she wanted to make mischief. The woman thrives on making mischief," Vanessa said, voice rising. "Lady or not, she is disliked in many circles as is Celia Holland. They are both vicious women and I am surprised, Theodore, that you are taking their side and not allowing me to give mine."

"Lady Palmer is highly regarded and I will not have you speaking of her like that."

"You never liked her either," Vanessa attempted a laugh. "Oh come on, Teddy, you yourself said she was an appalling woman."

"I should never have married you. I only did it to please Mama."

His face tightened and she knew then that it was too late for any more lies. She would not win him round. She had always known Lady Palmer was a gossip par excellence so it was surprising that she had kept her silence for so long. Perhaps she and Henrietta had had words and this was her way of getting back at the family, at two families indeed for she had told William's wife the very same thing.

"You regret marrying me?" her mouth was dry and it was difficult to speak. "But how can you say that? You love me, Theodore. You adore me. And I love you."

"You think that? May I acquaint you with the facts? I married you for many reasons, my dearest Vanessa, but love, not the kind of love you mean, was not one of them," he said and the words were cold, the distance between them a chasm.

"All right. I may have dallied," she said at last as the silence grew long and painful. She recalled her plan of action were this to happen and drew on that. "But William Whitlock was very persuasive and I was just silly to allow it. He mesmerised me, telling me I was beautiful. A woman likes to be told that," she said, recalling that he didn't often say it these days.

"The man is a bounder but then what can you expect from a mere mill owner? His wife is silly too but he was on his honeymoon and it was a despicable action. I shall not forgive him as I will not forgive you."

"It was only a kiss, Teddy, in the heat of the moment. There was a wonderful sunset and it was so romantic and he just happened to be at my side when you were not. If you had been there beside me it would have been so different. Surely you can see that, my darling?"

"Only a kiss?" he laughed out loud. "From what Lady Palmer says, it was a little more than that. There was passion in that kiss she says."

She could cheerfully kill Lady Palmer but of course the lady was quite right. As kisses go, the one with William would linger long in her head.

"Let me assure you, it will never happen again."

"I will not give you the chance, madam. I am divorcing you," he said. "I shall instruct my solicitor tomorrow. No..." he raised a hand as she made to protest. "Hear me out. This will be conducted discreetly and the staff at Snape Hall will not be aware of it for the time being. Nor will I see you destitute for I am a reasonable man but you can't expect much to come your way. You will have to throw yourself on the mercy of your lover. Take Charles with you."

"But Charles is your son. You only have to look at him."

"No he is not," he said, voice shaking, with anger or sadness she could not be sure. "Charles is Whitlock's son. You and I did not... we did not have intercourse during that holiday."

"We did," she protested hotly. "Maybe not on the steamer or the hotel in Luxor but we most certainly did on the way home at the hotel in France. You were fairly drunk but surely to goodness you remember."

"No, I do not," he said. "You told me we did but thinking back, I do not remember. And the child was conceived on that trip, on William Whitlock's honeymoon."

"But Theodore, that is not true. All right, I admit he kissed me that evening when Lady Palmer saw us" she said, feeling herself flush. "But, afterwards, we said goodbye and I hoped never to see him again. It wasn't my fault that you insisted on inviting them up to Snape Hall. I should have told you then but I knew you would take it badly and before you say it, nothing happened then either," she finished. "I wanted to tell you after Egypt but I didn't want any trouble. I thought you might challenge him to a duel," she added, trying belatedly for humour.

"I don't believe you and I will not listen to excuses," he said, holding up his hand. "I shall give you some time to collect yourself. You may go up to the Lancashire house, stay there until you find somewhere else. I will not throw you out although after the divorce you will have to find somewhere else to live. However, I do not want you to set foot in this house again. Neither you nor the bastard."

She was lost for words. Charles was his son. Yes, he looked more like her but she couldn't help that. And he did have the Asher chin. Henrietta had it. Theodore had it. And so did Charles.

"Now, get out..." he said, waving his hand in dismissal. "I have instructed your maid to pack all your clothes and the child's things that are still here. As for me, I never want to see you again."

She would not beg. She would not go down on her knees and beg.

Her marriage was over.

CHAPTER TWELVE

Back in the north, she needed to speak with William but it had to be done in public, in full view of the world so that they could never be accused of a secret assignation. She had therefore spoken with his secretary and arranged a very open meeting with him.

Walking towards The Royal Hippodrome in Friargate, she caught one or two glances, admiring and sometimes envious. Nobody here knew yet about the perilous state of her marriage but she knew that it would be all over London by now, a juicy bit of gossip. She would be discredited for Theodore would see to that but she was much more concerned about how this would affect Charles. Theodore had removed his name from the school he had so proudly entered him for, the school from which he would have gone on to Oxford and who knows what. Charles was a bright little boy and he could have done great things, things that were now denied him or at the very least made much harder.

She would fight her corner for him if not for herself.

"Vanessa…"

Her heart soared at the sound of his voice and she turned to face him, seeing his face light up. She knew she was looking her best, even though she was hardly feeling it, her hair was pinned up and her lipstick was a stunning red and she had used a few drops of perfume.

They greeted each other warmly as good friends do with a smile and a handshake for all the world as if it was just a chance meeting and William quickly brought her up to date with what was happening in his life. He had left his son Ashley in the capable arms of his nanny whilst Kathleen, who was slow in recovering, took a nap.

"Ashley?" Vanessa smiled. "So Kathleen got her way after all? She told me if she had a son he was to be called George William."

"Ashley George William."

"And how is he?"

"He's not strong either," he told her with a worried smile. "But the doctor says we must not worry because he did not have the best of starts in life. I am afraid Kathleen had a bad time with him. He was premature and only four and a half pounds but he's a fine little soul."

"I'm sure he is. Who does he look like?"

"His mother. He has a dusting of sandy hair already. I am afraid my father upset Kathleen by saying that he looks like the runt of the litter. I think he was just annoyed that he doesn't favour me."

"Did he really say that?" she gasped in annoyance.

"You've never met my father. I am afraid he speaks his mind to bishops or beggars alike."

She shivered, snuggling down into the fur stole she was wearing over her dark red two-piece. It was a chilly day for the time of year, grey clouds thudding over the sky as they weaved through the people milling about outside the theatre.

"This is a very public place," he said. "I was intrigued when I got your message. Delighted of course but I thought we had agreed not to meet."

"I have a present here for the baby, a good reason for us to meet."

"Thank you. What is it?"

"I have knitted a matinee jacket and bootees for him." She passed the small package over. "Please let Kathleen open it and give her my best wishes. Say we met by chance if you like."

"I will although she may wonder why you are giving the present to me and not her." He gave her a puzzled look. "I thought you two were friends. Didn't you visit before Ashley was born?"

So Kathleen had chosen not to tell him.

"I did but unfortunately your wife was taken ill and I haven't managed another visit. I'm afraid things did not go well at that meeting and I'm sorry to burden you with my problem but I don't know what to do. I don't know who to talk to. Theodore has practically thrown me out."

"What?"

"I am afraid Lady Palmer saw us on the deck of the steamer that night and has just decided now to tell Theodore, not directly but via an acquaintance. And I'm afraid there's more. The last time I saw Kathleen before the baby arrived, she told me that she too had seen Lady Palmer and been informed."

"She didn't say anything to me about it." He frowned. "But then she has been thinking only of the baby these last few months and her fear of having it. She has worried us all for she talked of nothing else. Lady Palmer eh?" He gave a low chuckle. "I can't say I'm surprised. She used to look down her nose at me. She was marginally pleasanter to Kathleen but I should think she was delighted to have something up her sleeve, something that would discredit me."

"It gets even worse. Theodore believes that Charles is your son," she told him, hearing his sharp intake of breath. "I told him the truth about that night but he chose not to believe me. I want you to talk to him, William. Please make him see sense."

"He won't listen to me. Surely you see that?"

"You can tell him straight. Man to man. Tell him that you and I... that we did not..." she struggled to say it as they walked slowly along, being jostled occasionally as people hurried by. Why were they in such a hurry? There seemed to be an edge of panic these days, people trying to fit things in before they were blasted to kingdom come. "Oh William, don't pretend you don't understand what I'm trying to ask you to do."

"I can't, Vanessa. I would if it would help but it would make things worse. If, as you say, Kathleen suspects there was something between us then we must make sure that we give it no credence. Particularly as she is so unwell..." he hesitated before shaking his head. "I think it might be best if we don't see each other again and perhaps it would be best if you keep this." He handed her back the present. "If nothing is said then nothing more will be made of it. I believe Kathleen has quietly and privately forgiven me and I hardly deserve it. I never meant to hurt her. I do love her, you know."

She nodded. She understood that.

"Not quite in the way I love you," he went on to say with a wry smile, voice a whisper. "There must be no more invitations to a house party but then the war will see to that, won't it?"

"Theodore will see to that," she said bitterly.

"I'm sorry."

She nodded, understanding his need to protect his frail Kathleen, especially important now that they had a son. She much admired his sense of duty but then he was an honourable man, never suggesting that they let this develop into an under-the-counter affair.

"What am I going to do, William? There's Charles to think of. If it were just me I would find somewhere to go, something to do but I have a child."

"Won't Theodore provide for him?"

"Why? I've told you, he doesn't believe he's his son."

"I can help you a little financially," he said. "And you can stay in one of the foreman's cottages if you get stuck. But I don't know how Kathleen will feel about that and I couldn't do it behind her back."

She laughed. "How do you think she will feel? Thank you for the offer but I couldn't do that. Theodore is giving me time and allowing me to stay at the Hall but I can't stay there for ever. Theodore has not visited in ages but I don't believe the staff know yet about the divorce."

"Divorce?"

"Yes. He's quite determined and his mother is backing him I'm afraid. She never really liked me. It was a little conspiracy between her and Mrs Crawford."

"Who is Mrs Crawford?"

"Nobody you know. A distant relative of mine," she said, holding onto the pretence as she had been trained to do. "I stayed with her when I came to London and she and Mrs Asher arranged that Theodore and I should meet. It was not love at first sight but we were suited apparently. The ladies considered it to be a good match."

"It's my fault," he said. "If I hadn't kissed you that evening, none of this would have happened."

"If I hadn't kissed you back, none of this would have happened."

They exchanged a look, a look that said clearly that for two pins they would kiss each other here and now and to hell with the consequences. There was this sizzling sensuality between them that was missing from each of their relationships with Kathleen and Theodore.

"Theodore's business is in trouble but Henrietta is bailing him out," she told him bluntly. "If only there hadn't been a war, he would have had his picture house contract but now he has to use his inheritance to prop things up. How is your business?"

"Booming. We are doing a lot for the war effort but of course I wouldn't wish it to be like that. It just is."

They slowed their pace, not touching, and Vanessa shivered a little, crossing her arms over her coat and hugging herself. They paused at the top of Lune Street looking into a shop window but neither of them seeing anything that was in that window. Seeing instead, their sombre reflections.

"I wish..." she said softly.

"You wish what?"

She shook her head and shortly afterwards they went their separate ways. Vanessa risked looking over her shoulder before she turned the corner, searching for a glimpse of the back of his head amongst the crowd, bumping into somebody as a result and having to offer an apology.

When she risked another look, he was gone.

CHAPTER THIRTEEN

The Blitz had begun in earnest with a massive air raid in London.

Up in the north, George Whitlock was dead and he had, in the absolutely final version of his Will left all the money, the Whitlock fortune, to the grown up children of a certain Harry Cookson. It did not take long for people to work out that Harry Cookson was the man killed in the horrible accident at the mill when, following the inquest, George Whitlock was held to be blameless.

Heads nodded then because by leaving Cookson's family all the money, George Whitlock had finally admitted he did hold himself personally responsible and they recognised it as a gentlemanly thing to do albeit a little late. The latest and last amendment to the Will, amended almost monthly in the past year, was, however, causing his solicitor Mr Hawkins of Hawkins, Hawkins & Newsham a headache.

Mr Hawkins placed a note in the local paper asking that the family of the late Harry Cookson contact him at their earliest convenience when they might learn something to their advantage.

***

"Where is she?" Vanessa asked Mrs Crawford who had picked up the telephone at once.

"Good morning, Vanessa, and if you are referring to your sister, Lizzie is not here," Mrs Crawford said in a slightly peeved tone, for Vanessa usually enquired first about her health. "After she's done the chores, off she goes. She likes to take a walk around the streets. She will be at one of the bombed out sites, just standing there watching the men at work clearing it and pulling out bodies."

"Good heavens." Vanessa gasped. "That's no place for her."

"She revels in it and I have to listen to such tales when she gets back. Her eyes shine when she talks of it. I despair of her sometimes, Vanessa, I really do. I've told her again and again that they do not want people gawping because they have work to do but she will not listen."

"She never does listen. I am sorry I left her with you. It wasn't fair of me."

"I said she could stay with me." She could feel Mrs Crawford smiling, knew that she did not hold it against her. "I feel responsible. Where else would she go?"

"She's my sister."

"Nobody must know that. We have come far, Vanessa, and we must stand firm. I am teaching her to play the piano and she has taken to it very well and is rather good, better than you, dare I say.'

Vanessa managed a laugh. "That's not difficult."

Mrs Crawford sighed. "I had a meeting last night and Lizzie wanted to come but I had to ban her from it because she would have been far too challenging to the spirits. She was most unhappy, kicking out quite disgracefully and I had to lock her in her room. I felt dreadful doing that but what could I do?"

"Did she behave then?"

"Oh yes. I am afraid I had to threaten her. I told her if she made a sound I would never let her play the piano again."

Vanessa understood for hadn't she done the same thing? Threatening to deprive Lizzie of something she loved was cruel but sometimes necessary.

"The meeting left me exhausted," Mrs Crawford continued. "And the spirits were so insistent, flooding through even before we had finished 'Nearer my God to Thee'"

Time to change the subject for, as the years went by, it bothered her more and more. Vanessa wanted to step back from the disturbing world Mrs Crawford inhabited and not just because of Theodore's views. She was still not totally convinced although just how it was done still evaded her.

"What is it like down there?" Vanessa asked. "How are you coping?"

"Theodore did the right thing in sending you north, my dear. You will be much safer there. As for us, we try to keep our minds off it. Lizzie refuses to go into the shelter though. She insists on playing the piano when the siren goes off. She says she is not frightened. She claims to have a charmed life."

"She believes it but you should go into the shelter yourself. If she won't then that's her fault. Don't put yourself in danger, Mrs Crawford. I could shake her but she's always had a mind of her own."

"If Lizzie has a charmed life and I am beside her then perhaps my life is charmed too and, as you know, I am not afraid of death. Don't worry, Vanessa, we will survive. In the meantime, Lizzie has been industrious making some dresses and she has gained a little weight and looks a lot better."

"Thank you for that. Does she know that Mr Whitlock has died? Have you told her about the money?"

"Oh yes. As soon as I heard from Mrs Flintoff, I told her to inform Mr Hawkins of Lizzie's whereabouts and we have had a letter from him which I read out to her. She was terrified at first when she saw it was from a solicitor because she thought it was a summons."

"For what?"

"She won't say."

"What did she say about the money?"

"She was quite unmoved although she did say it was no more than she deserved. She said she could buy a real silver bangle with it and would she have enough left over for a piano? She has no idea about the value of money."

"Does she realise that she's a rich woman now?"

"I have tried my best to explain. I've told her she must go back to Preston to claim the money and she says she will go when she's ready."

"I don't like you being in London. You could come up to me." Vanessa said realizing at once that was a silly thing to say as her own position at Snape Hall was not even secure. "You would be safe here."

"No. I have no intention of returning to Preston. This is my home and I have decided that if Lizzie won't go in the shelter, neither will I. I can't leave her alone, can I?"

"You must." Vanessa told her firmly. "There's no need for you to risk your life. Promise me that if the siren goes off you will go into the shelter no matter what Lizzie does."

"We shall see," Mrs Crawford said. "How are you coping, my dear? And how is the little man?"

"Charles is fine but I am not. So much has happened and I have to see you. I don't know who else I can turn to and I can't tell you this over the telephone. It's much too complicated."

"I don't want you visiting down here," Mrs Crawford said firmly. "You are to stay where you are. You are still up at the house in Lancashire?" She paused giving Vanessa a moment and then, as the silence continued, she carried on exasperated. "Please tell me what the matter is. The telephone is perfectly safe. Nobody is listening. It's just me. What is it? I know you don't care for the house up there but you are safe and you have to think of Charles."

"He's all I think about," Vanessa said quietly. "The truth is I may not be able to stay here much longer."

"What do you mean? What's happened, Vanessa?"

"Have you not spoken to Henrietta Asher recently?"

"Not for some time. We have drifted apart, a mutual agreement for, in truth, we never really got on."

"It's Theodore," she said. "He's taken against me and got it into his head that Charles is not his."

"My goodness, how foolish of him. How dare he suggest such a thing? How has it come about?"

"He accuses me of being unfaithful," Vanessa said. "When we were on holiday in Egypt before Charles was born."

"I remember. You met up with the Whitlock's, didn't you? And Theodore has got it into his head that you and William Whitlock were involved in an assignation? Am I right?"

"Yes. How did you guess?"

"I know you, Vanessa. And I know you still love him or think you do. I saw your face when Mrs Flintoff talked of him so it would not surprise me in the slightest if you had not flirted a little when you met him. Goodness, child, you can speak honestly with me. Did you flirt?"

"Perhaps." She said, remembering the sidelong glances from lowered lids, the little hidden messages in her eyes. "I didn't mean to," she added quickly. "And, as soon as I realised how dangerous a liaison might be, I put a stop to it. We both did. We were foolish I admit but we behaved impeccably afterwards."

Mrs Crawford drew a sharp breath. "How foolish? I need the truth, Nessa." Again the reverting to her old name came as a shock. "Is there any truth in this? Is Charles William's son?"

"No. On Maggie's grave, he is Theodore's. He has the Asher chin," she said, mystified that they could not see that when it was plain as plain. "Will you talk to Henrietta?"

"I think not. As I say, we have drifted apart and this sounds a very complicated affair and I fear that once Henrietta takes a stand she will not budge."

"Sorry, I shouldn't involve you and it would be hopeless anyway. He told me I could stay at Snape Hall until the divorce goes through and after that I have nowhere to go."

"You could come to me of course but I don't want you in London. I can let you have some money, just enough to keep you afloat but now that you find yourself in this predicament the obvious solution is to present yourself to the solicitor as a daughter of Harry Cookson so that you can claim your part of the inheritance. It will keep you and Charles comfortable for the rest of your life."

"How can I do that? I am not Nessa any more. My past is past and you always said I could never go back to it."

"No, that is true but these are exceptional circumstances, aren't they? Theodore is cutting you off without a bean and you have a child to care for. I never thought I would live to see the day but the fact is you no longer have anything to lose by admitting who you really are. And don't you think the money is richly deserved. George Whitlock has indicated that he was to blame, that in effect he killed your father and so, for your family's sake, you must accept your share."

"How will I prove I am who I say I am? It says Vanessa Asher on my identity card. It's as if Nessa never existed. We told lie after lie. We blotted her out completely."

Mrs Crawford sighed. "Exactly. You brought nothing with you other than a few scraps of clothing when you came to London with me. Even if you get a copy of your birth certificate, it will prove nothing. However, I can vouch for you and so can Mrs Flintoff although I don't believe she can be relied upon."

It was agreed that Mrs Crawford accompanied by Lizzie would come up to Preston. They would meet Vanessa and they would all go to see Mr Hawkins the solicitor to explain things. It could not happen immediately so she would simply have to sit tight and twiddle her thumbs for a little while.

***

Two weeks later the whole street was wiped out.

Mrs Crawford was pulled out of the rubble and taken to hospital in a grave condition but of Lizzie there was no sign.

Vanessa rushed down to London and thence to the hospital where she was told she could see Mrs Crawford for a few minutes. She had suffered internal damage and was not expected to live much longer. In fact, it was nothing short of a miracle she was still with us, the nurse explained in hushed tones, when you considered the extent of the injuries.

"Five minutes. She's very tired," she told Vanessa, drawing the curtains around the bed. Vanessa took a deep breath and edged forward, sitting down on a hard chair beside the bed.

"It's me," she said, voice steady after the initial shock of seeing her lying there, even paler if that was possible. Other than her colour, there was no outward sign of injury. "Auntie Florence, I'm here."

For a moment there was no response but then the eyelids flickered and she opened her eyes.

"What are you doing here? I told you not to come to London. You should be with your child," she said, the words spoken slowly and with a great effort. "Do you know where Lizzie is? She was playing the piano and I was there right beside her."

"They haven't found her," Vanessa whispered. She didn't want her sister dead but she didn't want her to have survived and be wandering around somewhere grievously injured. "Is she dead?" she asked, holding onto Mrs Crawford's hand. "Can you ask the spirits if it isn't too much for you?"

There was a fleeting smile. "Then you do believe, my dear."

Vanessa nodded. There was no harm in keeping her options open but just now, at this moment, she did believe.

"It's too soon for a message if she has passed." She drew a long shuddering breath and it seemed an age before she spoke again so that Vanessa looked at her anxiously, relieved when she saw the chest rise at last. "Forgive me."

Vanessa stilled her hand as a cold chill passed all around and a scent of flowers flooded the air as at a séance.

The nurse, rather forbidding with a smile as starched as her uniform, popped her head round the screen, took one look and then hurried to the bed. "It won't be long," she told Vanessa, drawing her aside and whispering. "Your mother is quite comfortable in no pain. Do you want to stay for a little longer?"

Vanessa, not bothering to correct her, nodded. She owed much to this woman although at the last she had separated her forever from her family. She had created a new life for her which maybe was about to crumble but at least she had given her a chance. Sometimes she wondered if Mrs Crawford had done it for her or for herself but what did that matter now?

Closing her eyes, she recited the Lord's Prayer, knowing it would be a comfort, holding on tight to her hand, waiting for them to come.

And, when the moment came, she felt it.

CHAPTER FOURTEEN

Mr Barker drove her to the solicitors' offices in Winckley Square. The secretary who greeted her gave her a funny look, almost a sneer before instructing her to wait in a sparsely furnished ante-room.

"Mrs Asher...?" The secretary was back, managing the thinnest of smiles. If she smiled her face would crack... her mum's unkindly words about one of their more miserable neighbours came thudding back and suddenly for some reason she was back to being Nessa again, missing her mum, missing Maggie, even Lizzie. It was being back in Preston that did it. It unsettled her much too much. "Mr Hawkins is ready for you. Would you come through?"

She had taken an age deciding what to wear today, finally choosing a pale yellow and white two-piece with her white buck-skin shoes, the overall effect smart but not too ostentatious.

The room across the corridor was warm and stuffy. Mr Hawkins was sitting behind his desk and, although he half rose to greet her, he remained there until she was seated opposite him.

"What can I do for you, Mrs Asher?" he asked in a reedy voice. "I understand you have information regarding the estate of the deceased George Whitlock."

She nodded, painfully aware of the absence of proof. Mrs Crawford could have vouched for her but Mrs Crawford was dead and Lizzie too. She had tried to contact Mrs Flintoff but had been stoutly rebuffed.

"I understand that the late Mr George Whitlock left an amount of money to the Cookson family..." she began, fingering her pearls, as she saw Mr Hawkins looking squarely at her in a manner that quite unsettled her. "I have to tell you that Harry Cookson was my father, Olive Cookson my mother. My sisters were Maggie, who died of pneumonia and Lizzie who is believed killed in an air raid in London, so I am claiming the inheritance for myself. As Harry Cookson's sole living relative, I believe Mr Whitlock would have wished it to come to me."

"I see. So, you are saying that you are Nessa Cookson," Mr Hawkins said with a sniff that managed neatly to convey his feelings. "And yet your identity card..." he waved a hand towards the small green document. "This tells me that you are

Vanessa Asher with a London address. How do you explain that?"

"Asher is my married name. We have a house in London and my husband's family also have a house at Chipping where I am staying at present."

"Why is your husband not here?"

"He doesn't know me as Nessa. He doesn't know my background."

"I see." Mr Hawkins clearly did not see and suddenly she saw it from his viewpoint. It was her word and her word only and why should he believe a word of it.

"It's a long story, Mr Hawkins" she began wearily. "After I left home, I was taken down to London by a Mrs Florence Crawford."

"Ah."

"Please listen," she implored, as desperation crept in for she could sense that this man's mind was already made up. "I lived with her for some time before I met and married Theodore Asher. I called myself Vanessa rather than Nessa on my arrival in London."

"Why?" The eyes were sharp.

"Because I..." she struggled to explain. "It was Mrs Crawford's idea. I was starting a new life away from here and it was simpler and more appropriate to become someone else. Calling myself Vanessa made me feel quite different. I became Vanessa Jones and we invented a new background for me."

"And where is Mrs Crawford now?"

"Dead," she said. "Her house suffered a direct hit. My sister Lizzie was living with her although they did not find her body."

Mr Hawkins drummed skeleton-thin fingers on the desk. "You are not the first person to come along..." he went on with the slightest of smiles. "My secretary has been inundated with letters following our piece in the paper. My client Mr Whitlock himself came out of the whole business very well. People admire his generosity and his family have been most dignified. But, sadly, there are always people on the make in this world, Mrs Asher. Women who come forward simply trying to claim something that they have no right to. I have seen more Nessa Cookson's this past month than I care to name."

"But I am Nessa. Ask me anything you like. I can tell you everything about the house that we lived in," she said. "Things that I would only know if I had lived there. There are people who might still remember me."

"I see. Perhaps we might solve this once and for all," Mr Hawkins said, ringing a little bell on his desk. "My clerk is waiting in the next room and he has someone with him. If anyone can recognise you, Mrs Asher, then I expect your sister Lizzie can and she is here."

"Here?" Vanessa gasped. "But I thought she was dead in the air raid."

"Precisely," he said as there was a tap on the door and a clerk came in accompanied by Lizzie.

Vanessa rose shakily to her feet, emotions spinning out of control.

"How on earth..." she began, transfixed to the spot as Lizzie looked at her.

"I survived," Lizzie said tonelessly. "It was a miracle they said. I was dug out but I only had bruises. I have a charmed life, you see. " She glanced at the clerk. "What is it you want me to say, sir?" she asked.

"I want you to tell me, Lizzie..." he smiled kindly at her. "I want you to tell the truth. I want you to tell me if this lady is your sister Nessa?"

Lizzie looked at her, long and hard, and Vanessa saw the glint in her eyes and knew.

"I've never seen her before in my life," Lizzie said.

***

Betty was in a terrible state. Now that bombs were falling, she was worried about what would happen if the German soldiers got their hands on her.

"You can get pills, madam," she told Vanessa, whispering the words as they sat in the nursery, whispering as if Charles could understand what she was talking about. "Pills that can kill you in seconds before anything can happen. I was wondering if you could get one for me, just in case. I've never been with a man," she added, blushing furiously. "I was saving myself for when I get married but I'd rather die than let a German have his way with me."

"Now, Betty, there's no need for pills," Vanessa reassured her. "It won't come to that."

They looked at Charles who, oblivious, was sleeping peacefully, his thumb in his mouth and exchanged a little smile.

"My mum wants me to go home," Betty carried on. "My brothers are gone to war and she has the twins to look after and she's not well and worried sick and she doesn't want to send them away to the country but they say they'll be safer there until it's all over."

"It was good of you to come up here with me, Betty, but it means you are far away from home. You must miss your mother."

"I don't mind. I love looking after babies. I love Charles."

"I know you do and I'm grateful to you for looking after him," Vanessa told her. "I'm sure he loves you too."

She nodded, pleased at that and Vanessa relaxed a little for the last thing she wanted was an agitated Betty fussing too much. Who on earth had started up this rumour about the German soldiers and the suicide pill? How dare they put silly ideas into silly girls' heads? But then, wasn't she once a silly girl herself and not so long ago either although so much had happened of late that she felt eons older. She was now a mother with responsibilities and it was weighing heavily upon her. The awful thing was that she may have to dispense with Betty's services soon for she could not afford to keep her, not when Theodore stopped paying her wages which he was doing at the moment, probably in error as nanny was simply included in the general wages.

Alone in the parlour later, she took the time to consider her position now that Lizzie had disowned her. It was no more than she deserved because Lizzie had felt abandoned and, ultimately, it was no surprise. She had known the minute she saw her sister in Mr Hawkins office that she would say what she had said. It was written in her eyes as clear as clear. She had always had this vindictive streak in her and Vanessa saw now that Maggie had been right and that there was no reasoning to be had, not with Lizzie.

After she was shown the door, she had done the only thing she could do, trying to hold onto some degree of dignity and exiting the office via the smirking secretary, going outside and climbing into the waiting car.

If Barker suspected something was wrong, he said nothing and the journey back was accomplished in silence whereupon she retreated to her parlour.

She could appeal to Lizzie's better nature but what good would that do.

She gave a deep shuddering breath. How had Lizzie escaped with cuts and bruises? Perhaps she did have a charmed life after all.

Tears at her predicament were threatening and she took out her handkerchief and gripped it tightly for she could not succumb to them.

What was she going to do?

She couldn't keep up the pretence to the remaining staff here, not for much longer, although the Barkers would stay to look after the Hall long after she was gone. She doubted that Theodore would ever come here again but it would remain in the Asher family as it had done for generations.

It should have been Charles's inheritance.

"He's your son," she said out loud, clenching her fists and banging them on the arm of the chair. "He's your son, Teddy."

***

A few days on, she thought of the one man who could help, the one man who could vouch for her, the man who knew her as Nessa Cookson.

Tony Walsh. She had no idea where he was or if he was still alive for there were many casualties reported each day in London. She knew she had disappointed him by not loving him as he loved her but, if he did still love her, then surely he would help. After all he had been good as his word and not said a word to anyone about her deception and he could have gained a lot by doing so.

She felt she could trust him.

Her excitement quickly faded as her attempts to contact him came to nothing with nobody in the newspaper world knowing of him. Had he lied to her? If so, that made two of them for she had told so many lies to so many people that this surely was her punishment.

His mother! Of course, Tony's mother might still be around, still at the old address. She could vouch for her for she would remember her and, if she would, it would be worth the humiliation of going there.

***

"Nessa Cookson. Well I never." Ada Walsh stood on the doorstep, older but recognizable as the formidable woman who had shouted the odds at them when they were growing up. She had shrunk over the years but still had a steely glint in her eyes that showed no signs of softening as she looked Nessa up and down.

"May I come in?" she asked, trying to modify her accent and not quite succeeding for she caught the woman's raised eyebrows. "Please."

She followed Ada into the house, a childhood memory surfacing of being part of a little gang standing here with Ada wielding a wet cloth round their grubby faces and hands before giving them a biscuit or a jam butty if they were lucky and shooing them off again.

"If you want to know where he is, I don't know and if I did, I wouldn't tell," Ada said. "Sit down. Do you want a cuppa?" she asked, northern hospitality cutting through the hostility.

Vanessa shook her head. "I'm sorry..." she muttered. "I've been to see the solicitor about the Whitlock will and he doesn't believe I'm Nessa and

Lizzie said I wasn't her sister. I thought Tony might tell them who I really am or perhaps you… you know who I am, don't you?"

"I do but why should I help you?" Ada laughed. "You broke my son's heart, lady, and your poor mother's and I'll not forgive that. You never came back for the funerals. Too hoity toity to do that."

"I couldn't." She held onto the accusing gaze. "I really couldn't but that doesn't mean I didn't think about them. Maggie, my dad and my mum."

"Funny way of showing it."

"Do you really not know where Tony is?"

"He said he'd let me know but he hasn't, not yet." She sniffed. "All I know is that he's gone to America. Got himself an American girl, a nice enough lass. He wanted to marry you but you knew better, didn't you?"

"I didn't love him," she said softly. "You can't make yourself love somebody."

"Oh yes you can. It needs a bit of work but you can do it. What do you need that money for anyway? You've got more money than you know what to do with. Look at your clothes," she said, crossing her arms round her bosom, her pinafore crisp and clean.

It was no use.

"When you hear from him tell Tony that I hope he's happy," she said, standing up and picking up her gloves. "I wish him all the best, tell him that. And I'm very sorry."

"Not as sorry as me, lady. I know you have a little lad yourself now. How would you feel if somebody broke his heart?"

Ada Walsh showed her the door.

CHAPTER FIFTEEN

Early strolls in the fresh country air offered some solace over the next few weeks but on her return to the house one morning, she was met by Mrs Barker, a worried looking lady at the best of times but just now she was wringing her hands in agitation.

"Oh, madam, I didn't know where you'd got to. Mr Barker's just got back and he's left her there at the station. I thought it was a rum do giving her a lift in the first place and I told him as much but would he listen."

"Left who? There's no need to upset yourself," she smiled. "Mr Barker has my permission to use the car for short journeys, sparingly of course."

"No, madam, you don't understand. She had a bag with her, you see, and when I've gone up to the nursery, she's packed a bag for little Charles too. She's taken him and that daft husband of mine has helped her. He didn't think there was anything wrong. You see, he told me that she was meeting Mr Asher from the train, that Mr Asher wanted the little lad to meet him off the train but why then did she tell Mr Barker to come back here if she was meeting the master? It doesn't make sense but he was too gormless to cotton on. I could string him up myself, I honestly could. When I think of that poor little mite, I could cry."

"Betty?" It was dawning what Mrs Barker was talking about, bit by bit as if her thoughts were in slow motion. "Betty's gone to the station and taken Charles with her?"

"That's right." Mrs Barker looked relieved that her shambled message had now got through. "She's kidnapped him."

Vanessa was already flying up the stairs to the nursery asking Mrs Barker to get Mr Barker to bring the car back round. She saw at once that Mrs Barker was right. Betty had taken some essential items with her, a change of clothes for the baby, napkins, creams and things and Betty's clothes, few of them in any case, were gone too.

***

"Stop saying you are sorry, Barker, and just get me there. The London train doesn't leave until 3 o'clock so we might be in time if you hurry up."

She had never known Barker drive so fast and she was out of the car almost before he stopped, tearing into the station, her ankle-strap shoes with their chunky heels hardly the right footwear for running.

"Platform ticket, madam?"

"Let me through. It's my baby. She's kidnapped him," she yelled and, seeing her face, hearing the authority in her voice, she was let through at once.

To her relief Betty was standing there on the platform holding Charles, gripping him tightly, expression changing as she saw Vanessa bearing down on her.

"Madam... I can explain. I love him," she said, clutching him tighter. "He's my little soldier and he loves his Betty. It's me who cuddles him at night when he's upset. You never come near. You're all right, snuggled up in that big bed but it's me who gets up and sorts him out and he knows it. He knows who loves him most. He'll be all right with me and my mum. We know how to handle babies."

"Give him to me," Vanessa hissed, reaching out and snatching a now crying child from her. "You are dismissed and you are lucky you don't find yourself in prison for this."

Betty stood before her, empty handed, shocked, face white, wearing her best coat, one Vanessa had given her, a herringbone mix of green and black, a quality coat that Vanessa had tired of. She was doing it now, donating unwanted clothes to staff, just as Lizzie had been given that beautiful green frock all those years ago. This coat hung loosely on thin Betty but she was proud of it, clutching it to her now as they heard the train steaming in and people around them began to pick up their belongings.

"Oh my Lord, you won't get the Police, will you?" Betty muttered. "Don't turn me in, madam."

Steam filled the platform, hissing as the train came to a halt.

"Get on that train and don't let me see you ever again."

"But who'll look after him when I'm gone," Betty said, tears beginning to spill from those big brown eyes. "Who'll get up in the night when he cries?"

"I will." Vanessa clutched him close, a heavyweight now, smoothing down his hair under his bonnet, feeling his little chest heaving as his sobs eased. "I'm his mother. I will do it."

"You'll never do it," Betty huffed, in a final touch of defiance. "Not a lady like you. You don't have the first idea of looking after a baby."

"Get on that train before I call the Police," Vanessa said, quiet now so as not to alarm the distressed Charles too much. There was so much she wanted to say to this girl but there was no time. She liked Betty but would never forgive her this. "Go to London and don't ever come back because if you come near Charles again, I will turn you in."

She took the bag from Betty, the one containing her child's things, watching as Betty climbed on board, making sure she did not get off again, waiting until the train steamed out of the station. She saw Betty through the window, mouthing sorry, waving but, hitching Charles further into her arms, she turned away.

There were a few looks her way from people who had witnessed the commotion but she ignored them.

"There, there, darling," she whispered, kissing his baby-fat cheek. "Mother's here. You're safe now."

He struggled just a bit but then, tired, he flopped against her.

It seemed her heart was only just returning to its normal steady beat but, as she made her way towards Barker who was waiting for them, she had never been as happy as this, not in a very long time.

Charles was smelly, she realised, on the way home but that would quickly be remedied and she would move up to the nursery tonight so that she was near him if he awoke.

"I always thought she was a wrong 'un," Barker said. "But Mrs Barker is right, I should have known she was up to no good."

"No harm done," Vanessa told him, feeling sure that his wife would be waiting with a few harsh words.

"After all, "he went on, not quite finished. "The master doesn't come up here these days, does he, so I might have known it was a rum do?"

"He has business to attend to in London," she said shortly, not wanting to go into that.

"Nor Mrs Asher," he continued, meaning her mother-in-law. "I trust the lady is well, madam?"

"Oh yes, very well, thank you."

Charles was heavy on her lap, long lashes covering his sleepy eyes. She thought of Henrietta, his grandmother, who would never know him. Perhaps one day when his baby features became firmer, the likeness to his father would be more pronounced and then perhaps there would be an apology, a plea for forgiveness.

But could she ever forgive?

***

Vanessa was in the hall when she heard the knock on the door and she went to answer it herself, something that would have infuriated Theodore.

214

Seeing who was standing there, she then tried to shut the door but Lizzie was too quick by half. She was past her before she could help it.

"I don't know how you've the brass neck to come here?" Vanessa exploded. "After what you did to me? And how did you know where this house was anyway?"

"I know things," she said, eyes gleaming with mischief. "Don't I just? I just asked about and everybody knows the Asher's and where they live out near Chipping." She glanced around, sniffed. "This is a grand place but it's too big for me. I'm buying a house and I shall advertise for a lady companion. She can wash up and stuff, and sit and listen to me playing the piano."

"Is everything all right, madam?" The maid, a chirpy little thing, appeared, flustered and a little late in the day, looking at Lizzie curiously. Lizzie, in turn, looked at her as if she had just discovered her underneath a flat stone, her disdain remarkable and such that the maid flushed and gave a little bob.

"Yes thank you. Miss Cookson is visiting. Perhaps you would bring us tea, Maisie," Vanessa said, opening the door to the sitting room. "Sit down," she said and Lizzie did so eventually after the usual rigmarole. She was tidy, clean, her hair brushed, wearing a dress and coat that fit her.

Bizarrely, she was also wearing lipstick and powder. In spite of the uneven application, she looked heaps better, quite presentable in fact.

"I haven't got the money yet," she said. "But I will have it soon. Mr Hawkins gave me what he called an advance to tide me over. I've bought new clothes and I've come here by car."

"You shouldn't have come. What if I were to ring Mr Hawkins now and tell him you are here. Wouldn't he think that odd?"

"I would be gone by the time he got here and that man worships the ground I walk on. I think he might ask me to marry him but he's only after my money and he's not getting any of that." Lizzie said, looking round the room. "This is nice."

From his perambulator in the room she had turned into a day nursery, Charles cried out and Vanessa excused herself, noticing that Lizzie was following her.

Outside the door, she stopped dead.

"You may see him," she said, keeping her voice level. "But, if you ever harm a hair of his head, Lizzie Cookson, I'll kill you. Is that clear?"

"Harm him?" Lizzie laughed. "Why would I do that? I like babies."

They entered the dimly lit nursery where Charles had settled himself, fast asleep in his cot, sprawled on his back, his covers kicked off and gently, Vanessa drew them up round him once more and tucked them in.

"Is that him?" Lizzie asked in an awed whisper, peering down. "Is that my nephew? Big lad for his age, isn't he?"

"Yes," Vanessa said proudly. "He likes you to sing to him. Betty, his old nanny, used to sing to him and I sing the same songs. He likes that."

"Did you sack her?"

"She had to go back to London to be with her mother," Vanessa said, declining to go into the details.

"Tell you what..." Lizzie reached down and gently touched him. "I'll look after him. He won't need a nanny when he's got his Auntie Lizzie," she continued gently stroking his leg, her face tender. "Hello, little lad," she said.

Vanessa looked at her, at the baby, and made a decision.

"Would you like to hold him?"

"Can I? All on my own?"

"Didn't I promise you could one day? Sit over there in that big chair, sit well back, and I'll bring him to you."

Lizzie did as she was told, immediately, sitting expectantly there, feet dangling, arms at the ready.

Vanessa bent over the cot and lifted the little boy out. Sleepy, he did not protest but at once cuddled in close to her as he used to do with Betty and she kissed his cheek, explaining to him – how silly for he had few words – that his Auntie Lizzie was waiting to hold him.

"Hello, baby," Lizzie said softly, looking up at Vanessa in wonder. "I've never held a baby before. She never let me. She said I'd drop it. But I won't. He's safe as houses with me."

They sat together a while, quietly, Lizzie holding the baby who seemed perfectly content in her arms. His confidence was enough for Vanessa. Lizzie loved this child. Lizzie would do him no harm.

"Shall I take him?" she asked at last. "Let's put him back in his cot and then we'll go and have our tea and talk."

"Talk?" Lizzie looked up, that sudden suspicion leaping in her eyes. "What about?"

"Us. Me and you."

Gently, she took Charles from her sister's arms and settled him back in his cot. She smiled as he let out a little baby sneeze before closing his eyes.

"He's not taking bad, is he?" Lizzie asked, alarmed at the sneeze.

"He's perfectly well," she said, not as nervous now about his health for he was indeed a sturdy little fellow. Theodore had called him that and the memory upset her but she sniffed it away for there was no time for that.

"Do you have a piano?" Lizzie asked, following her back into the sitting room.

"Yes. I don't play very well."

"I do. Mrs Crawford taught me," Lizzie said. "Can I stay here, our Nessa, until I get sorted out? I can buy a house when I get my money and you can come and live with me then. It's my money," she added. "But I might give you some."

"I don't want it," Vanessa told her, leading her out of the room. "I have enough," she added defiantly wishing it was true.

"I might have a cook," Lizzie said. "And I shall buy myself a real silver bangle, a fur coat, and a piano. Can I stay here until I get my house?" There was a pause and Vanessa dared look in her eyes, seeing something there that she couldn't quite puzzle out. Lizzie had never had a chance in life, dismissed and backed into a corner.

"All right, you can stay with me for the moment," she said. "But I don't want people knowing you're my sister. We can say you're an acquaintance, a distant cousin. Miss Elizabeth Cookson, a distant cousin who is staying for a while. I'll teach you to speak properly."

"Shan't," Lizzie said bluntly. "I talk how I talk. And I am your sister. Like it or not."

"Yes, but..." Vanessa let it pass. Lizzie would not change. She would always be Lizzie. And yes, she could no longer deny that she was her sister although what Mr Hawkins would make of that she could not imagine.

"Is that husband of yours going to divorce you then?" Lizzie asked, taking a lace handkerchief out of her pocket and giving her nose a most unladylike blow.

"How do you know that?"

"Auntie Florence told me when I asked her. She told me how you wanted the money for yourself."

"I just wanted my share. After all, dad didn't deserve to die like that and it killed mum too."

"Is the baby William Whitlock's?" Lizzie persisted.

"I don't know what you mean."

"You met him again when he was on his honeymoon. Nine months before Charlie was born. So... is it his son or your husband's?" She paused as there was a knock at the door and Maisie entered with the tea tray, casting a curious yet respectful glance towards Lizzie who in turn continued to look at her as if she was something the cat had dragged in. When she was gone, she carried on. "So, who is Charlie's father?"

"My husband," Vanessa said firmly, hiding her surprise for she had thought the ways of the world, the ways of married life, had escaped Lizzie. "I did meet William again but we did nothing wrong. We are both married and we didn't want to do anything to upset Theodore or Kathleen. We were never meant to be together."

"But you want to be together? You still love him?"

"I do". She raised her eyes for what was the point of trying to fool her sister who did indeed know everything. "And he loves me, too, but even though I will be divorced soon he is still married and it will stay that way. We have decided not to see each other again."

Lizzie nodded, taking a biscuit and eating it, crumbs flying everywhere. "That's a shame," she said. "You could be happy with him, happier than you were with your husband and it would be nice for me to visit you if you lived at Ruby House. Just think, you would be the mistress and I would be the grand visitor coming in the front door and taking tea."

"It will never be. Look, Lizzie… why don't we try to make the best of things? Wherever I go after this, you can come and see Charles whenever you like and we can be friends."

"Friends? You and me?" Lizzie stared at her, mulling it over. "Do you mean it? Do you want to be friends?"

"Why not? It's better than being enemies. We are sisters, Lizzie. We should love each other, although you've made it hard for me to even like you disowning me like you did."

"I had to. That money's mine," Lizzie said. "I'm not sharing it. You went off to London with Auntie Florence. You don't need it."

It was a waste of time trying to explain to Lizzie that she did in fact need it. Of course she needed money... but she was not going to beg, not from Lizzie, not after the way she had treated her. It would be a long time before she could forget the look on that secretary's face as she had been shown the door. It was as near as being thrown out physically as she had ever come to and the door had indeed been slammed behind her.

"We'll never be friends, you and me, not when you look at me like that." Lizzie went on, surprisingly perceptive as she interpreted the look of despair cast her way. "You don't love me and you don't trust me, do you?"

"Haven't I just said? You don't make it easy for me, Lizzie."

"What would it take to make you change your mind? What would it take for you to love me like you loved our Maggie?"

Vanessa shrugged, biting at her lip for she did not want to think of Maggie.

"Suppose I do something for you, something that you really want, will that make us proper friends? Will you love me then?"

"What are you talking about? Are you going to give me some of the money after all?" Vanessa asked with a small smile.

"Oh no. That's mine." she said with that grin of hers. "You aren't having a penny. No, I'll think of something that will make you very happy. We should be friends. Maggie would be pleased. She always wanted us to be friends."

"Well, yes..." Vanessa glanced at the clock. "You'd better stay. You can have Betty's room..." although even as she said it, she wondered if that was wise, putting Lizzie right next door to Charles.

"Don't worry. I won't harm him and I'll kill anybody who does," Lizzie said, reading her mind. "I love Charlie. I'm going to buy him something when I get my money. A teddy bear from his Auntie Lizzie."

CHAPTER SIXTEEN

Now that Mrs Crawford was gone, she had lost contact with Mrs Flintoff but the servants' grapevine was strong as ever and Mrs Barker knew the housekeeper at Ruby House and so gossip was still trickling Vanessa's way.

Kathleen Whitlock was having more fits and was very frail, spending her days reclining on the chaise-longue in the drawing room, retiring early to bed and barely talking to anybody, including William.

"That man is a saint to put up with it," Mrs Barker told Vanessa, her indiscretion knowing no bounds. "Mr Barker says she needs a kick up the backside. Mind you, they do say the little lad is flourishing but she shows no interest at all in him."

"I am sorry to hear that but if she is feeling poorly then we have to forgive her."

"It doesn't matter how poorly you are feeling, a mother always looks after her own," Mrs Barker said firmly.

***

The verdict was accidental death.

Kathleen Whitlock's medical history was well known and documented and it was assumed that she had taken one of her turns at the top of the servants' stairs and fainted, falling the full length of the cruelly hard stone steps, although it was the final one, the edge of the final step, that had done the dreadful deed and gashed her head open.

Vanessa, of course, did not attend the funeral.

**

"I have decided I want a house with six bedrooms," Lizzie said, the day of the funeral, when Vanessa's thoughts were with William. "And a big drawing room for entertaining."

"Entertaining?" Vanessa laughed. "You have nobody to entertain, Lizzie."

"I will have," Lizzie said. "When people see I have money, I will have."

"Do you want me to help you look for a house?"

Lizzie beamed. "I'd like that. Are we friends now, our Nessa?"

"Can't you call me Vanessa? It will confuse Charles unless you do," she said, knowing that to be a good enough reason, for Lizzie was genuinely

225

fond of him and he responded to her. She had caught the pair of them the other day in a giggling heap.

"Vanessa..." Lizzie said carefully, rolling the word on her tongue. "All right. I will if I can remember. Are we friends now? I've done something for you so we should be friends now."

"What have you done?" Vanessa asked, looking at the clock, thinking that by now poor Kathleen would be buried in the Whitlock vault, next to her father-in-law. She had sent a letter of condolence but she had not spoken to William, not yet, and would give him time to come to her if that is what he wanted to do. She felt no gloating for this, not when a little boy had just been deprived of his mother. She did not want Kathleen dead, although now there was no longer any barrier to her and William being together, although thinking such a thought today of all days made her feel desperately ashamed.

"I pushed her down the stairs for you," Lizzie said, clambering onto the piano stool and setting up the sheet music.

It took a moment to dawn.

"But she fell..." Vanessa said, feeling her heart thud. "She took a turn and fell down the stairs."

"No, she didn't." Lizzie started to play Run Rabbit Run. She played by touch but liked to pretend she was reading the score. The notes were perfect. "I pushed her."

Vanessa reached over, yanked her off the piano stool and caught her arms.

"Tell me you didn't?" she said. "You're lying."

"Get off me. You're hurting me," she said, rubbing at her arms as Vanessa, horrified, let go. "I talked to Emily Kershaw."

"Who's she?"

"She works in the scullery up at Ruby House." Lizzie said. "I've promised her she can have a job when I get my house. I'll pay her more and give her more time off. She'll have to call me Miss Cookson though."

"You talked to Emily and then what?"

"She said Thursday was Cook's day off and there would be nobody in, except the nanny who stays upstairs in the nursery and can't hear proper anyway, so I crept in by the back door..." she grinned.

"But you've never been to the house."

"I have. I went to get mum once when Maggie had one of her bad dos and I went in the back door and round to the servants' stairs."

"I see."

"I crept in and called out her name... Kathleen... and Mrs Whitlock came down the hall and I hid behind the door and then she came out again and walked to the top of the stairs and just stood there holding onto the rail and I crept up behind her and I pushed her. She went rolling down and down, all the way, banged her head. I went down and had a good look but I knew she was a goner in a minute or two. She didn't know who I was. Just stared at me, she did."

"Oh my God...!" Vanessa put her hand to her mouth, felt herself sway with the horror of it. "You killed her. Lizzie, you killed her."

"She didn't have long to live anyway. Them fits of hers were getting worse and she was getting frailer. She was going to die. Auntie Florence always said as she was going to die young. She was going to suffer for years and get weaker and weaker." Lizzie said defiantly. "I did her a favour."

"She could have got better, Lizzie. The doctors could have done something for her."

"No, they couldn't or they would have done something before," Lizzie said and there was a certain logic in that. She looked at Vanessa and, when she spoke again, her voice was soft and gentle, the voice she used on Charles. "Don't fret, Vanessa love. I did it for you, so that we can be friends. You can marry him now, you see. And you can go to live at Ruby House just like you've always wanted. I'm never going to marry," she added. "But they never gave me a chance. They said I was simple and I always knew I wasn't."

Vanessa sat down heavily on the nearest chair, trying to gather her wits together, listening to this new quiet reflective voice.

They stood, inches apart, and it was Vanessa who looked away first, hearing Lizzie's skirt rustle as she returned to the piano and started to play a bright and breezy tune.

Looking at the back of her sister's head, Vanessa felt a deep sorrow circling and trapping her. Lizzie could be hanged for this if they found out. Lizzie, whose mind worked in such odd ways, who had tried, in her own way, to sort things out for her. That signified some sort of warped love, a love that had never shown itself except in anger and aggression.

"Oh, Lizzie love, what have you done...?"

In despair, she stood close behind her, seeing the fingers flying over the keys. Nice hands now they weren't submerged in washing-up water all day long.

She knew she would never tell anybody about this. Never. She could never betray her own sister. Even if it meant putting a lid on her own happiness, she could never ever do that.

"Come on, join in..." Lizzie stopped and turned. "Sing. Come on, Vanessa, sing..."

She started up again and, with the vision of Kathleen hurtling down those stairs to her death, Vanessa, mouth dry, somehow managed to start to sing.

"Yes, we have no bananas,
We have no bananas today…"

Lizzie half turned and grinned at her but there was no malice this time, just sheer happiness.

"We have roast beef and onions…" Lizzie sang out, her voice raucous but in tune.

Tears welling up now, Vanessa carried on as the piano tinkled out its merry tune.

Her heart was broken, for Kathleen, for William, for Lizzie.

And for herself.

***

With her spirits lifted, Lizzie relented at last and presented Vanessa with a substantial cheque to cover her share of the Whitlock fortune.

She made sure that Lizzie's purchase of her house, a large property in Watling Street Road went ahead smoothly and, as well as Emily Kershaw who was coming in to clean, she engaged a companion for her, a middle-aged lonely widowed lady, who, like Lizzie, adored music.

"My sister..." Vanessa had long since given up the pretence because it no longer mattered. "My sister needs looking after, Mrs Rigby."

"I know, my dear." She smiled. "And I will do that. I know how to handle ladies like her."

For herself and Charles, she bought a much smaller property in Ashton and settled into building a cautiously happy life for herself and her son. She had no idea yet what she would tell him as he grew older and started to ask questions for it was hard to explain that his father had abandoned them as he had. She was more puzzled now than angry with Theodore for his intransigence. He had not listened. He had not believed her but then, over the years, she had told so many lies, come to believe some of them that it was hardly surprising.

And, as he grew older and lost some of his baby plumpness, Charles began to develop a distinct look of Theodore that even Theodore would find it hard to denounce. It made her wonder if she should march him down to London, confront his father, but then she wondered if that is what she wanted. Even if Theodore forgave her, she was not sure she would ever forgive him.

CHAPTER SEVENTEEN

She met William Whitlock again by accident as they reached simultaneously for the pair of gloves in the haberdashery department of the shop in Fishergate.

"Sorry, madam… oh…"

They stared at each other, each holding one of the gloves, before laughing self consciously and dropping them. He intended them for a birthday present for his sister Martha, he explained, just as she intended them for a birthday present for her sister Lizzie.

"You have a sister?"

There was so much to say after that and he took her to the Kardomah café where, over tea and crumpets, she explained everything, watching his face as he listened intently.

"I am so sorry to have deceived you," she said at last. "It was a terrible thing to do."

"I knew I had seen you before," he said triumphantly. "But I could never bring it to mind. It was just a fleeting moment, wasn't it? For a while after that I hoped you would appear in the house although I knew of course that you were far too young and innocent and my father would have killed me if he knew I had such evil thoughts. And then seeing you again on the steamer that evening, you just took my breath away and Kathleen knew. She was very young but she was not as naïve as she liked to pretend."

"She was always very kind to me. I liked her."

"I have missed you, my sweet." He took hold of her hand but the café had partitions for privacy and there was nobody to see. "And now we are free, both of us, and if you were really Vanessa and not Nessa I might well ask you to marry me."

She bit her lip. It might have been a mistake to tell the truth but she could not live a lie with him and of course she could not expect him to marry her now, now that he knew who she really was.

And then he laughed, his eyes suddenly merry and she remembered that he had a sense of humour, something totally absent in Theodore and that he had been merely teasing her.

"Don't you realize that it doesn't matter?" he said. "It's been a shock I have to admit but it doesn't matter at all. In fact, it makes me love you all the more. Will you marry me, Vanessa, Nessa, whoever you are? Of course we're still in the middle of this infernal war but we mustn't let that stop us. It will end soon."

"Will it? Look, I have to go home. I've left Charles with Lizzie and I said I wouldn't be late back."

"Is he all right with her?" He frowned. "After what you've told me about her, I'm not sure you should leave him with her."

"He's fine. She loves him," she said.

She had told him everything about her past, her father whipping her, going to London with Mrs Crawford, losing Maggie, marrying Theodore, even told him about her father's accident and his father's part in it.

"We knew of the accident but father strenuously denied there was anything wrong with the machinery and, although I was suspicious, I had to accept that. I am so sorry, Vanessa. So very sorry but it will never happen again. Now I am in charge, if an accident occurs, it will be a true accident."

She nodded, accepting that.

"Thank you for being honest with me," he went on. "We shouldn't have secrets, you and I."

No.

But there was still one secret she would have to hold onto; Lizzie's part in Kathleen's death.

***

"You haven't answered my question," he said, as she got up to leave.

She shook her head. "No. I'm sorry, William, but the answer is no. I can't marry you."

"Why not?"

"Kathleen is barely cold in her grave," she told him. "Please show some respect, William."

She could not tell him the truth, the words that would condemn Lizzie. Would you still want to marry me, my darling, she wanted to say, if you knew that my sister killed your wife?

She knew that would be the end of it, and it would land poor Lizzie in all sorts of trouble; probably condemn her to life in the asylum for ever.

**

Lizzie had stayed overnight at Vanessa's, sleeping in the bedroom beside Charles and next morning, she brought Vanessa a cup of tea saying that Charles was still fast asleep. She knocked lightly on the door and walked in and these days there was a distinct bounce in her step, none of the shuffling of old. Vanessa was noticing it more and more, a lightening in her mood, an outer display of happiness that was reaching inward where even that sly look was gone, replaced by a genuinely merry look. As for Charles … well he idolized her.

"William has asked me to marry him," Vanessa told her, reaching for her bed-jacket and slipping it round her shoulders. "I said no."

"Why? You are daft. You know you love him so what's up?"

"You know perfectly well what the matter is. How can I marry him when you...?" she looked round anxiously, not daring to say it.

Lizzie laughed. "Oh, you mean, me saying that I pushed Kathleen down those stairs? Is that all that's worrying you?"

"All?" Vanessa sighed and sipped her tea. "I can't marry him, can I?"

"For heavens sake, I didn't kill her," Lizzie said, sitting first at one chair and then the other for she didn't seem to be able to break that particular habit. "As if I would do such a thing. Honestly, Nessa Cookson, you would believe anything. You should know me by now. It's all talk with me. It always was."

"Why did you say you did?"

"When I read in the paper..." she could read now and had learnt surprisingly quickly under Mrs Crawford's tuition. "When I read she was dead I thought I'd tell you I'd done it so that we could be friends."

"Oh, Lizzie…" she sighed. "Maggie always said she couldn't make head or tail of you and neither can I."

"Nobody could but nobody tried. I wanted people to notice me, not ignore me and that's why I used to say those awful things because they did notice me then. They were all frightened to death of me. I used to walk down the street and folks would point at me and talk about me behind my back. I was somebody. I was that daft Lizzie."

"So, you're now telling me that you didn't push Kathleen down the stairs?"

"I am."

"I'm sorry, Lizzie. I want to believe you but how can I be sure?"

"You can ask Emily Kershaw if you like. She was there that afternoon, upstairs somewhere with her boyfriend. And, after they'd done what they were doing, she'd gone downstairs to the kitchen and seen Mrs Whitlock coming through to the servants' hall and she didn't want Mrs Whitlock asking questions. And then she saw her dropping down as she fainted and she heard her fall down the stairs and she was so frightened she ran back upstairs to her boyfriend and pretended she hadn't seen and heard it. And when she heard nanny making a fuss she got rid of the boyfriend, shoved him out of the back door, got dressed herself and nobody was any the wiser. And that is the truth. This time that's the truth and you can like it or lump it."

She so wanted to believe her. Looking at Lizzie's shining eyes, she so wanted that.

"Oh Lizzie, why did you have to make up such a cock and bull story? What are we going to do with you?" She opened her arms wide, raising relieved eyes to the ceiling, and, to her surprise, Lizzie shot at her like a bullet and huddled close.

***

She needed to make sure though so, on a day when she knew Lizzie would be out, she called round to the house in Watling Street Road. Emily answered the door, looking petrified as Vanessa explained that no, she was not visiting Miss Cookson but wanted to speak to Emily about something important.

Vanessa took charge taking the girl through to the sitting room which now housed Lizzie's pride and joy; a brand new piano.

"Sit down, Emily." She smiled encouragingly. "You are not in any trouble so don't worry. But I want you to tell me about the day Mrs Whitlock fell down the stairs at Ruby House? Tell me the truth. Were you there?"

"It wasn't my fault," Emily Kershaw said, cheeks bright. "We were upstairs, me and my boyfriend..." her cheeks became even brighter. "We knew there was nobody about because madam wouldn't come up there and the nanny was in the nursery with the baby and she doesn't hear very well so we had a bit of time to ourselves. We never get any time to ourselves, Mrs Asher. There's nowhere for us to go. My Tom's a good man and we're going to get married. He's not in the best of health which is why he hasn't been called up but he's as brave as the next man."

"I see." Vanessa stopped short of clicking her tongue, remembering what it was like to be young and in love. "Miss Cookson told me that she was there at the house that day. Is that true?"

Emily shook her head. "No. I told Miss Cookson what I'd seen and she said that if you asked me I was to say she was there and I wasn't but that doesn't make sense, does it? The thing is I couldn't tell anybody because I would have lost my job."

"Go on."

"Well... begging your pardon, Mrs Asher, but afterwards Tom said he was hungry and I said I would see if there was a bite to eat and so I went downstairs and I don't know if she heard me... Mrs Whitlock that is... but next I know she's up there at the top of the servants' stairs and she sees me standing there in my shift." She shuddered at the memory. "But she just said that she felt faint and could she have a cup of tea? And then..." she put her hand over her mouth. "Before I knew it, she's at the bottom of the stairs and... oh Mrs Asher... I knew the minute I looked down at her that she was gone."

"So you left her there?"

"I had to. I had to get back upstairs and tell him and then get him out of the house and me too before anybody saw us. We couldn't help her."

"Thank you, Emily. You've been honest with me."

"Thank you, madam. It's been bothering me because it's not right for me to tell lies. What are you going to do? I don't want to lose my job. I like Miss Cookson and she's nice to me. Are you going to turn me in?"

"Goodness no." Vanessa half smiled for hadn't poor deluded Betty said the same thing. It was good to have the truth confirmed but it didn't make her feel any better for not believing Lizzie in the first place. From now on, there had to be some trust between them. She trusted her with Charles and that had to be good enough.

***

For her second marriage she wore an emerald green dress with a new diamond pin in her lapel. Martha and Lizzie were present, Martha holding Ashley and Lizzie holding Charles. Wearing William's ring at last, after all this time, should have felt wonderful and it did but what heartache it had taken to get to this point in her life.

That evening, following the afternoon wedding, they had a modest reception for they could not afford to be seen to be over lavish at a time like this and sometime in the evening Lizzie was persuaded to play for them.

Holding her breath, William holding her hand, Vanessa watched as Lizzie fussed herself onto the piano stool. There were a few smiles for nobody believed she would be any good at it but as her hands touched the keys a collective breath of delight soared through the room.

Lizzie was a natural. All her favourites; Roll out the Barrel, Run Rabbit Run, Bless 'em All and to her credit even Martha Whitlock unbound sufficiently to join in the singing.

***

Vanessa had asked that they should have a different bedroom from the one William had shared with Kathleen and this one was smaller, to the side of the house, but very pleasant with a view of the park through the trees. Late that night she cuddled in close to her new husband and sighed. "I'm so sorry about Kathleen. You must be thinking of her now, William. No, no, it's all right," she added as she saw he was about to protest.

He squeezed her hand, moving gently against her. "I was thinking of her. She was far too young but she loved me and she loved Ashley although she didn't like to show it."

"Of course she did. Ashley is growing into a fine boy and I will do my best to be a good mother to him. I have to do that for Kathleen. I owe her that. He and Charles will be good company for each other as they grow."

"They are lucky little boys. Two aunties, Martha and Lizzie. I like Lizzie," he said. "She's so uncomplicated."

Vanessa stifled a laugh for Lizzie was the most complicated soul she had ever known but she would not disagree with him, not tonight, for this was the beginning of everything.

About the author…

Patricia has been writing for 30 years. Born and brought up in the north of England, she has lived in various parts of the north (both east and west of the Pennines) before moving to Devon in 2004 to be nearer her family and also because she loves the area. Patricia loves walking on Dartmoor and is a volunteer at a National Trust property, Buckland Abbey, where she enjoys soaking up the atmosphere and meeting the visitors.

Her first published work was a children's novel followed by romance novellas before she began writing longer fiction for the women's market. Her novels are centred on the family where she loves to explore the differing personalities within a family and how that sometimes leads to conflict and problems. She likes to give her characters a fairly free rein and does not plan too much but always has an overall view of what the story is going to be about.

Her short stories are sometimes darker and she still has not cracked the murder/mystery genre but is working on that.

Her latest novel 'What Friends Are For' is published as an e-book by Cloudberry Fiction at Lusciousbooks, available on Amazon.

What Friends are For
Elaine, Toni and Zoe of Long Lane in Morecambe Bay have become friends through a babysitting circle. Despite their different personalities, they are drawn to each other in the hope of finding support amidst increasing family pressures. As each is faced by their respective family problems, each family being under strain, their friendship is put to a test. What are friends really for – and can their friendship survive?

Further titles by Patricia Fawcett available from Amazon.

Follow Patricia's blog on her website at www.patriciafawcett.co.uk

Printed in Great Britain
by Amazon